Welcome Home, Mary Anne

Other books by Ann M. Martin

Leo the Magnificat
Rachel Parker, Kindergarten Show-off
Eleven Kids, One Summer
Ma and Pa Dracula
Yours Turly, Shirley
Ten Kids, No Pets
Slam Book
Just a Summer Romance
Missing Since Monday
With You and Without You
Me and Katie (the Pest)
Stage Fright
Inside Out
Bummer Summer

THE KIDS IN MS. COLMAN'S CLASS series
BABY-SITTERS LITTLE SISTER series
THE BABY-SITTERS CLUB mysteries
THE BABY-SITTERS CLUB series
CALIFORNIA DIARIES series

written with Paula Danziger:
Snail Mail No More
P.S. Longer Letter Later

Friends *Baby-sitters Club* Forever

Welcome Home, Mary Anne

Ann M. Martin

AN
APPLE
PAPERBACK

SCHOLASTIC INC.

New York Toronto London Auckland Sydney

Mexico City   New Delhi   Hong Kong

No part of this publication may be reproduced in whole or in part, or stored in a retrieval system or transmitted in any form or by any means, electronic, mechanical, photocopying, recording, or otherwise, without written permission of the publisher. For information regarding permission, write to Scholastic Inc., Attention: Permissions Department, 555 Broadway, New York, NY 10012.

ISBN 0-590-52346-5

12 11 10 9 8 7 6 5 4 3 2 1   0 1 2 3 4 5/0

This edition printed and bound in Canada
5 4 3 2 1   DW   0 1 2 3/0

The author gratefully acknowledges
Ellen Miles
for her help in
preparing this manuscript.

Welcome Home, Mary Anne

✿ Chapter 1

What was it Dorothy said? *There's no place like home.* She clicked her heels three times and repeated that phrase, and suddenly everything was all right again. She was home in Kansas, with Auntie Em and Uncle Henry.

I wish I could click my heels three times and be home. But there's a problem. And it isn't just that I don't have ruby slippers. It's this: I don't know where home is anymore. Or what it is.

Is home where your friends are? Well, then, I guess my home is Stoneybrook, Connecticut, this little town where I've spent most of my life. If a town can be a home, this one is mine.

Is home your family? That makes it tougher. First of all, my family's pretty tiny. It's also spread out. Some here, some in California, some in Iowa.

Or is home the house you live in? Hmmm. If that's what it is, no wonder I'm confused and feeling more than a little lost. Because if that's the case, Dorothy's magic can't take me anywhere.

I don't mean I'm homeless. No, I'm lucky enough to be living in a perfectly nice house in a nice neighborhood. And tomorrow (tomorrow!) I'll be moving into a new house, a house built just for my family and me.

So what's my problem?

Good question. My problem is that I'm not sure that the new house will feel like home. What I want right now is to feel settled, grounded, sure of who I am and where I belong. And I may be wrong about this, but I'm fairly certain that's what home is all about.

Whew! Am I sounding too deep here? Maybe I should lighten up and start over again.

My name is Mary Anne Spier. I'm thirteen years old and in the eighth grade at Stoneybrook Middle School, or SMS. I have brown hair and brown eyes and I'm on the short side. I'm shy around new people, but I like to think I'm a good friend to people I know. I've been told I'm a good listener. I'm sensitive, and I cry easily. I like kittens (I have a gray tiger-striped one named Tigger), old movies, rainy days, strawberry ice cream, and hot chocolate with marsh-mallows on snowy winter afternoons.

And I feel very mixed-up and rootless. . . .

It's hard to get away from that fact. Maybe I should just explain. What happened was, my house burned down. To the ground. We lost just about everything.

Who's "we"? Well, the people living there at the time were my dad, Richard, my stepmother, Sharon, and me. Sharon's kids from her first marriage, Dawn and Jeff, were in California at the time. They live there with their dad, though they do visit us on vacations. (In fact, they're due to arrive here soon, but more about that later.)

I was very attached to that house, even though I didn't grow up in it. I only moved into it when Dad married Sharon, which wasn't so long ago, but it had felt like home to me.

It was a lovely old farmhouse, filled with history and with the vibrations (please don't think I'm weird) of all the people who'd lived there in the past. I don't mean ghosts, although there was one of those too. I just mean I always had a strong sense that the house had been a home to dozens of people before I arrived.

And, as I said, it was a home to me too. Partly

because it was a family place. For most of my life my family consisted of just two people: my dad and me. My mom died soon after I was born. I never knew her. And I didn't know what it was like to have a mom.

My dad deserves two tons of credit. He did a wonderful job of raising me on his own. Except for a few months right after my mom's death, when he was just too full of grief to see straight and he sent me off to live with my grandparents (my mothers' parents, that is) in Iowa. I didn't even know about that until recently. For a long time my grandmother was not part of my life, but now she is again, which is wonderful. She visited us recently and brought along all kinds of mementos of my mom to replace the things we'd lost in the fire. That meant a lot.

Anyway, there we were, my dad and I, for years and years. Then I met Dawn Schafer, who'd recently moved from California to Stoneybrook with her brother, Jeff, and their divorced mom. Dawn and I became best friends. We soon discovered that her mom and my dad, who had both grown up here in Stoneybrook, had been high school sweethearts. We brought them back together, they fell in love again, and my best friend became my stepsister. Sigh. Isn't it romantic?

After the wedding, Dad and I moved in with Sharon and Dawn. (Jeff never took to Connecticut and moved back to California to live with his dad even before the wedding.) We'd just begun adjusting to our new family constellation when Dawn decided she belonged back in California too. That was a hard idea to adjust to. But I did, though I still miss her a lot. Anyway, now it's just Dad, Sharon, and me.

I love Sharon. She's great. She may not be as tidy as Dad and I are, or as organized (unless you consider it organized to keep your car keys in the fridge/potted geranium/whatever spot is handy). Still, she's a wonderful stepmother. But she's not my mom. My mom died a long time ago.

So.

Sharon and Dad and I were burned out of the farmhouse and had to figure out what to do next. For awhile there was the possibility that we might move away. Dad had a job offer in Philadelphia, and Sharon wanted to go back to school; so it looked as if we might be leaving Stoneybrook.

Happily, that didn't happen. Instead, we settled for awhile into a temporarily available house on the street where I'd grown up, next door to one of my oldest friends, Claudia Kishi. We hired a contractor to create a new house for us out of the barn that had stood next to the farmhouse (it had survived the fire). Then we waited. And waited.

Now our new house is ready. And tomorrow is moving day. I'm packing up the few things I own — some borrowed, some salvaged from the fire — and getting ready to go home.

I hope.

My friends will be there to help: Claudia, Stacey McGill, and Kristy Thomas. Kristy's my best friend from before either of us could say much besides "more milk!" She and the others have been there for me through a lot: Dawn's moving away, the fire, and my breakup with Logan.

Logan.

I haven't mentioned him, have I? Well, Logan Bruno was my boyfriend for a long time. We were a great couple and destined to be together forever. Everybody thought so. Everybody but me. I broke up with him not long ago.

Why did I break up with the sweetest guy at SMS? Well, I'm not sure if I can explain, but it had to do with feeling the need to have my own identity — to be Mary Anne instead of just part of MaryAnne-andLogan. Has that happened yet? To be honest, the answer is no. That's another reason I feel unsettled. I miss Logan. I miss how easy it was to be with him, to be part of a couple.

I sound like a mess, don't I? It's not so bad, really. It's just that I feel up in the air about a lot of things.

Here's another example. Those friends I mentioned? We all belong to the Baby-sitters Club, or BSC. Actually, we *are* the club, and that's a new development. There used to be more members. But the BSC has been through a lot of changes recently. Kristy's still president; that will never change, since she came up with the idea for the club. But our membership has shrunk to four, and while we still take on plenty of baby-sitting jobs (that's the club's purpose), we aren't actively advertising for business. And we don't meet as regularly as we used to. The BSC was a huge part of my life for a long time; its changes just added to my lost feeling.

The fact is, our new house is awesome. It's huge and full of light and open spaces. The furniture in it is brand-new, and I got to help pick it out. What do I have to complain about? Not a thing, really. Having a new house — a new *home* — is going to make me feel grounded, strong, sure of myself.

Right?

Or will I feel like a stranger in my own house?

As I was wondering about that, I heard the phone ring downstairs. "Mary Anne!" Sharon called a few seconds later. "It's for you."

"Thanks!" I called back as I stepped into the hall to pick up the extension. "Hello?"

"Hey, it's Kristy."

"Hi," I said. "What's up?" It felt good to hear her voice. I'd been dwelling on my feelings for too long.

"Just checking in. How's the packing going?"

I laughed. "It's done. There wasn't much to it."

"I guess not," Kristy said. "Sorry I wasn't there to help."

"That's okay. How did the Krushers game go?"

It was late June, which meant that Kristy was caught up in softball. She coaches a team called Kristy's Krushers, made up of little kids in the neighborhood. They have a blast.

"It was awesome. Jackie Rodowsky made the most incredible catch to end the game in extra innings. See, the score was tied two-two. The other team was up, with two outs. The count was two and three when Buddy hit one down the left-field line, and — "

Smiling, I let Kristy ramble on, spouting numbers

and baseball terms that meant nothing to me. Some things never change. Kristy will always be Kristy, full of energy, ideas, and enthusiasm. And she'll always be my friend, even though we couldn't be more different.

I knew she was psyched about helping me move, and so were Claudia and Stacey. Having them there would definitely help me feel as if I were coming home. And in a few days Dawn would be there to complete the picture.

Maybe I didn't need those ruby slippers after all.

Chapter 2

Saturday, June 27

Dear Diary,
Moving day! Finally.
I can't believe it. I
woke up at 5:30 this
morning and couldn't
go back to sleep. So
I've just been lying
in bed, wondering
how it will feel
tonight to lie down
in a new bed, in a
new house. My house.
Will it feel like
home? I hope

"Mary Anne!" my dad called.

I put down my pen and shut my journal. "Coming!" I replied. He didn't have to call me twice. Suddenly, I was starving. It was time for breakfast, time to start the big day. I pulled on a T-shirt and shorts and padded downstairs in my bare feet.

"Morning, honey," said Sharon. "Sleep well?" She gave me a quick smile as she bustled around the kitchen, packing up a few final items.

I shrugged. "I was up early," I said.

"We were too." My dad had just come into the kitchen, carrying a box marked ODDS AND ENDS.

Odds and ends. That was about all we owned anymore. Almost everything in our house had been destroyed by the fire. We'd salvaged a few things, but what can you really do with one half-burned shoe or a waterlogged book?

Friends and family had donated all kinds of things: clothes, kitchenware, even houseplants. You can't imagine how strange it is to realize your favorite African violet was destroyed by a fire. That's how it was, though, in the weeks after the fire. Every so often I'd be walking around, not thinking about much, and I'd remember yet another thing — *My favorite picture of Cam Geary on the beach! That note from the tooth fairy, congratulating me on my first lost tooth! My green velvet scrunchie!* — that had disappeared without a trace.

But it was time to forget about all that. It was time to move on, to face a new life with new things.

"Mary Anne?" my dad asked gently. "Are you okay?"

I smiled at him. "Sure," I said. "I'm excited about today, aren't you?"

He nodded. "I sure am. Why don't you grab something to eat and then we'll head on over?"

Our plan was for the three of us to drive to the new house early in the morning, to check things out. Furniture had been delivered during the last few days, and we needed to make decisions on its placement. Then we'd return to the rented house and start moving our boxes. That's where my friends were going to help out.

I fixed myself a bowl of cereal. Sharon offered me a fresh peach to slice over it. (She's a vegetarian and into that "five servings a day" thing about fruit and veggies.) "One less thing to pack," she said as she handed it over. I sat down at the table and watched as she finished packing a box labeled SPICES, UTENSILS, CANNED GOODS. Blithely, she slipped in three shoes (a pair of sneakers plus one high-heeled pump), a set of wrenches my dad had been using to work on his bicycle, and a jar of apricot facial scrub that had somehow found its way into the kitchen.

As I may have mentioned, Sharon is organizationally challenged. There were undoubtedly some surprises in store for unpacking time. I pictured myself opening a box labeled BANK STATEMENTS only to find Tigger inside. I suppressed a giggle.

"What's so funny?" Sharon asked, smiling at me.

"Nothing," I said, jumping up to rinse out my bowl. "I'm ready. Can we go over there now?"

"Yup," said my dad, glancing at his watch. "In fact, we should hop to it. People will be arriving here to help in just over an hour."

We piled into the car, taking a couple of boxes with us (I also brought my pillow; don't ask why), and headed for our new home.

"One seventy-seven Burnt Hill Road," I said as we pulled past the mailbox and into the driveway. "Same address, different house."

Sharon nodded. "Isn't it strange?" she said, sighing.

We were gazing through the car windows at what used to be the working barn for an old family farmhouse. It still looked a little like a barn. It was a big squared-off building with weathered siding. But now huge windows were everywhere, complete with window boxes brimming with pink and purple petunias. (Sharon was responsible for that homey touch.) And the house that had stood nearby for so long was gone. Vanished without a trace.

Well, maybe not quite without a trace. I could still see where the grass was greener, newer, in a large area near the barn. The area where our house had stood. But the landscapers had done an excellent job of cleaning up the yard and making it look as if the barn, and only the barn, belonged there.

"Well, what are we waiting for?" asked Dad. He opened his door and climbed out of the car. Sharon and I got out too.

"Which door?" I asked. The house was still so new to us that we hadn't figured out which entrance would be the one we used regularly. There was a front door with a knocker and a doormat. There was a back door too, which opened into the herb garden the landscapers had planted. But my favorite door was the one that opened wide. The old barn doors had been huge, big enough to let a horse and carriage through. Now those doors could slide open to show off our beautiful new kitchen. We'd soon be able to eat around the table with those doors wide open, looking out at the old apple tree I'd always loved.

The tree I'd stood under as I watched our house burn down.

I sighed. My memories of the past seemed all mixed up with my excitement about the future. I wanted to love my new house, but it wasn't easy to forget the old one.

"Let's use the front door," said Dad. "I want to check the new key I had made."

I followed Sharon and Dad up the new flagstone walkway, noticing the creeping thyme that bloomed purple between the stones. The landscapers had told me it was fine to step on it in order to enjoy the spicy smell it released. "It's a tough herb," I remembered hearing. "It can take it." Still, I felt funny tromping on the stuff. I walked carefully, carrying my pillow clutched to my stomach.

Dad's key worked, and the door swung open. "Well, here we are," he said. We walked inside, looking around. None of us had been there since the carpenters had cleaned up. We'd seen the place take shape over the last few months, but it had always seemed like a construction zone, full of sawhorses and lumber and smelling of paint.

"Wow," said Sharon.

"It's beautiful," I said.

It was. The sun shone through huge windows. The smell of freshly cut wood filled the air. The floors and woodwork gleamed, and the white paint was spotless.

"Look at the curtains in the breeze," Sharon said softly.

The curtains we'd picked out billowed lightly away from the dining room windows, catching the sunlight. They were beautiful gossamer curtains with a special touch: small pockets sewn in rows, translucent pockets that could hold a leaf, a dried flower, a cluster of berries. Sharon and I had spent lots of time over the last weeks collecting the prettiest things we could find to fill those pockets, and now I could see just how wonderful they looked, silhouetted by the sun. It would be fun finding new things to add to the pockets each season.

"Lovely," murmured my dad. "You two did a great job in here."

"You helped too," Sharon reminded him. "You picked out the couch, remember?"

She gestured toward the living room. We could see it without moving from where we stood, since the first floor of the barn is one huge open space. Dining room near the kitchen, living room at the other end.

(Oh, okay, the bathroom has walls. But that's it.) Amazingly, the living room felt cozy even with the open plan and the high ceilings. An off-white couch, huge and comfy, sat welcomingly across from a small cobalt-blue woodstove we would use for extra heat in the winter. A matching armchair, big enough to seat two people, sat near it at an angle. A rag rug in deep shades of purple and scarlet made the area seem warm and inviting. I could just imagine curling up on that chair to watch an old movie. A side table stood at one end of the couch, where I could keep my box of Kleenex. (I always bawl when I watch old movies. That's part of the fun.)

"I'm going up to my room," I announced. Carrying my pillow, I headed up the staircase, noticing again the polished maple wood of the stairs and banisters.

Upstairs were four bedrooms. Two of them were big: one for Sharon and my dad and one for me. And two of them were smaller, for Dawn and Jeff. Since neither of them would be living here full-time, that seemed fair. Sharon and Dad had their own bathroom adjoining their room, and there was another in the hall near the other three rooms. That would be all mine (yahoo!), except for when Dawn and Jeff were here.

I loved my room. It was spacious and full of light, like the rest of the house. I'd chosen a blue-and-yellow color scheme (two of my favorite colors) for a fresh, clean look. Sharon had helped me shop for curtains, a bedspread, and a rug. My new bed was comfortable, and I had a new desk for homework. The closet was huge, especially considering that I didn't have many clothes to fill it. I pictured myself in the room, doing homework on a winter evening. My desk lamp would cast a warm glow as snowflakes danced outside.

I put my pillow on my bed, arranging it just so. I hoped Tigger would curl up next to it that night, as he usually did. And in a flash I remembered how Tigger had woken me up that awful night of the fire. I shook my head to make the memory go away. I wanted to create new memories in this new house, not hang on to the old ones. This was an opportunity for a fresh beginning. I would have to start noticing new things. The sooner I did that, the sooner I'd feel at home here.

I heard Dad and Sharon walking around downstairs. It was probably time to head home to pack up the van we'd rented. I took one last glance around the room, adjusted the pillow again, and walked out, closing the door behind me.

Sharon and Dad were talking about ideas for re-arranging the furniture slightly in order to fit in the few items we'd be bringing over. They broke off when I came down the stairs. "How does your room look, sweetie?" asked my dad.

"Great," I answered. "The whole house looks great."

"It does, doesn't it?" He put one arm around me and the other around Sharon. "Welcome home," he said.

❀ Chapter 3

Home. I leaned my head against the car window. It was Monday morning, a couple of days later, and Sharon and I were on our way to the airport. In just under an hour, I'd be reunited with my stepsister and best friend. I was excited.

I was also tired. Despite my father's "welcome home" wishes, and despite the fact that our new house was beautiful, comfortable, and perfect in every way, I still didn't feel at home in it. For one thing, I wasn't able to sleep. I'd tossed and turned for most of the last few nights.

What was missing? Why couldn't I just relax and accept that I was home? I would lie in bed, wide awake, thoughts drifting. Images of our old house would spring into my mind. I pictured the front porch where I'd spent so much time reading in the hammock, the kitchen where Sharon had first shown me how to make a tofu burger (still not my favorite food), my cozy little bedroom.

I also thought about the house where I'd grown up, the one my dad and I shared for all those years. I even thought about my grandmother's house in Iowa. I'd never had any trouble feeling at home anywhere else. Why was it so hard now?

"Penny for your thoughts," Sharon said, glancing my way while we waited for a light to turn green.

I gave her a weak smile. "They aren't worth a penny." It was silly to feel this way and I knew it. I had no cause for complaint. I was ashamed to even tell Sharon what I was thinking. "Do you think Dawn's plane will be on time?" I asked, changing the subject.

Sharon nodded. "I called before we left the house," she told me. "According to the airline, everything's on schedule."

"Great," I said. "I can't wait to see her and Jeff."

"I can't either." We drove in silence for a moment. Then Sharon cleared her throat. "I guess this visit will be a little different for all of us, with Sunny coming," she said.

I felt a little twinge in my stomach. "I guess." I hadn't thought much about it, maybe because I didn't want to. But the fact was, this visit *would* be different. Dawn and Jeff weren't the only ones arriving on that plane. Dawn's California best friend, Sunny Winslow, would be on it too.

I've met Sunny. And I like her. She's smart and fun and has a lot of energy. But this time I was a little nervous about being around her. "Do you think she's still really sad?" I asked Sharon.

Sharon let out a sigh. "I do," she said. "It hasn't been that long since — "

"I know," I said quickly. Sharon didn't have to spell it out. And of course I knew Sunny would still be sad. After all, her mom had died. That's what Sharon had been about to say.

I'd heard a lot about Mrs. Winslow's illness and death. Dawn had been very close to Sunny's mom, so it had affected her deeply too. She'd talked about it a lot during our phone calls. It sounded *horrible*. Mrs. Winslow had had lung cancer, and she was in a lot of pain before she died. During the worst part of her illness, Sunny and Dawn were having friendship troubles, but they made up just before Mrs. Winslow died. And I have the feeling they're closer than ever now. They've been through a lot together — stuff I can't even imagine.

Mrs. Winslow was at home when she died. Dawn had a chance to say good-bye, which I know meant a lot to both of them. And Sunny was with her mother when she died.

Okay, the truth? I was nervous about Sunny's visit for a couple of reasons. One, because of her mom's death. I wasn't sure what to say to her or how to act. I lost my mom too, but since I don't even remember her, it's really not the same. Was Sunny going to cry all the time? Be extra sensitive about things? Was she going to want to talk about her mom? It was a little scary.

Two, I felt jealous of how close Sunny and Dawn must be after going through that experience together. I mean, I know Dawn doesn't live here anymore, and our friendship has changed because of that. We're still best friends, but in a different, long-distance kind of way. It was going to be hard to see her with her *real*, everyday best friend. Where was I going to fit into the picture?

Sharon somehow sensed what I was thinking. She reached over to pat my hand. "Everything's going to be all right," she told me gently.

"I hope so," I answered. "I guess Sunny really needed to get away, didn't she?"

Sharon nodded. "She has a lot to sort out. That's why her dad asked if she could come here for a month. Your dad and I thought it was a fine idea."

"So do I," I said, trying to sound more certain than I felt.

"I know it's a little daunting," said Sharon quietly. "But all she really needs is for us to welcome her and let her know we're here for her. There's not much else anyone can do right now. She has a lot of healing to do."

I looked at Sharon. Her hands were gripping the steering wheel tightly..I guessed she must be nervous too.

"What kind of things do you think Sunny will want to do?" I asked. "I mean, she's never been East before."

"Well, let's see," Sharon answered. "She'd probably like to see the ocean, just so she can compare the Atlantic to the Pacific. And we can take her on hikes, since the woods here are really different." She paused. "But I bet she'll mostly just want to do whatever you and Dawn are doing. You know, swim at the pool, go to movies, hang out at the mall."

I visualized the three of us doing those things. "Sure," I said. "That'll be fun." Again, I was trying to sound certain. Would Sunny be bored? I had the feeling California was a lot more exciting than Connecticut. We don't have huge waves for surfing or long boardwalks for in-line skating. There aren't many movie stars here. Even our food is boring. I remember visiting Dawn in California and eating all this exotic Mexican and Asian food, or stopping at a smoothie stand for a mango-papaya shake. Here it's pretty much pizza, burgers, fries, pizza, burgers, and fries.

I sighed.

"Don't worry so much, Mary Anne." Sharon shook her head, smiling. "It's going to be fun. Wait until Dawn and Jeff see the house. Don't you think they'll love it?"

We chatted for awhile about the house. Sharon had plans for expanding the herb garden, and she wanted my opinion. Before I knew it, we were pulling into a spot in the parking garage at the airport.

We found our way to the right gate and waited for Flight 326 to land. "There it is!" I said, pointing to a plane that was taxiing toward the long, moveable tunnel attached to Gate 7. "They're here!"

It took a long time for the plane to pull up to the gate. Then it sat there for awhile. Finally, passengers began to trickle through the tunnel.

We watched from behind a glass wall. Only passengers were allowed past the doors that opened into the gate. So when I saw Dawn and called her name, she couldn't hear me. "Dawn!" I yelled, waving. "Jeff! Sunny!" Normally, I'd be embarrassed about making such a scene. But I was so excited about seeing Dawn that I just didn't care. Suddenly, all my doubts and fears disappeared. Dawn looked like the same old Dawn, with her long, pale blonde hair and blue eyes. It was going to be great to have her here for a whole month.

Finally, she looked right at me. She gave me a huge smile and waved back. Then she touched Jeff on the shoulder and pointed to where we were standing. Sunny had already spotted us. She was smiling too — but only with her mouth, if you know what I mean. Her eyes looked sad. Sunny's pretty, with strawberry-blonde hair and freckles. She looked the same but different, if that makes sense.

When they came through the doors, Sharon and I were standing right there. Dawn and I flew into each other's arms, while Jeff let Sharon hug him (he's ten and not big on sentimental stuff). Then I turned to Sunny. "Welcome to Connecticut," I said. I gave her a hug too. She hugged me back.

"Thanks, Mary Anne," she said. "It's good to be here."

"And we're very happy to have you," Sharon said. Now it was her turn to hug Dawn and Sunny. I saw her give Sunny a long look as she held her by the shoulders. A look that said, *I'm so sorry*. Sunny looked back at Sharon. How did she manage not to cry? But Sunny's gaze was steady.

"I am totally psyched to be here!" she said as we headed for the baggage claim. "I want to see everything and do everything. I've never been *anywhere* before." See what I meant about Sunny's energy? She's always up for anything.

"Why would you *need* to go anywhere?" asked Jeff. "California's the best." He glanced at Sharon. "Sorry, Mom."

"That's okay," Sharon answered, shaking her head. "I know I raised a California boy. But you have to admit there are things you like about Connecticut, Jeff."

"Sure," he answered. "Especially in summer, when my friends are on vacation and we can fool around all day." He turned to me. "How are Nicky and the triplets?"

"They're fine," I said. Jeff is good friends with

the four Pike boys, brothers of an honorary BSC member — and good friend — named Mallory. "They can't wait to see you."

"We're going to build a rocket this summer," he announced, "and figure out a way to launch it. We've been working on the plans by e-mail."

"Great," said Sharon. "Just — "

"Be careful," Jeff said, in a singsong voice. "I know, I know. That's what Carol says too."

I glanced at Sharon. Carol is Dawn and Jeff's stepmother. She and their dad just had a new baby daughter, Grace. I know Dawn wasn't crazy about Carol at first, but I think they've become a lot closer. Carol is close to Sunny too. She was really there for Sunny during the time that Mrs. Winslow was dying, according to Dawn.

Sharon didn't seem to mind. "Well, Carol's absolutely right," she told Jeff. "Now, let's find your bags." We watched as suitcases began to tumble down a chute and ride around on a conveyor belt.

"There's mine!" said Sunny, reaching for an oversized black duffel.

"And mine," Dawn said, grabbing the backpack next to it.

Jeff's suitcase — an old brown one of his dad's that Jeff won't part with — tumbled down next.

"All set, then," said Sharon, leading us toward the door. "Ready to go home?"

Dawn and I exchanged a glance. I wondered if she felt the same way I did about "home." After all, she'd spent at least as much time in the house that had burned down as I had. It might be just as hard for her to get used to the idea of living in the barn.

"Ready as I'll ever be," said Dawn, shouldering her pack. "Let's go."

✳ Chapter 4

"Wow."

That's all she said. Dawn stood by the car, her backpack near her feet where she'd dropped it. She was staring at the barn.

We'd pulled up just moments ago, and Dawn and Jeff had climbed eagerly out of the car. Now both of them seemed frozen where they stood. Sunny didn't seem to notice. She bounded up the walk, dragging her duffel bag behind her. "Cool house," I heard her say to Sharon. "I love all the windows. They must let in a lot of sun."

"Dawn?" I asked. "What do you think?"

"I don't know what to think. I'm still not used to the idea that we're living in the barn."

"It is a little strange," I admitted. "I mean, think of all the things we used to do in the barn: hold BSC parties, run our summer day camp, swing from the hayloft — "

"Not to mention ghostbusting in the secret passage," Dawn put in.

"How could I forget?"

We smiled at each other. Dawn had always been thrilled about having a ghost of our own. I, on the other hand, was a little less delighted. Still, I had to admit it had been cool to know that the secret passage between the house and barn had once been used to hide slaves escaping via the Underground Railroad.

"Remember when — " Dawn began.

"Nicky was hiding in the passage and we thought he was a ghost?" I finished her thought. That was Nicky Pike, Jeff's friend. He'd gone through a phase of needing a place to hide out, and he'd chosen the secret passage. The noises he made scared us half to death before we figured out the truth.

She grinned. "How did you know that's what I was going to say?"

I shrugged. "I just knew." Dawn and I shared some pretty important history. And I could tell it was hard for her to see that a huge piece of that history — our house — had vanished. In its place, another piece of history, the barn, had changed completely. I put a hand on her shoulder. "The new place is great," I said quietly. "I think you'll like it, once you get used to it."

"I won't!" Jeff spoke up. "I hate it. I hate that our stupid house had to burn down in a stupid fire."

He was kicking at the grass as he spoke. We were standing in the area where the grass was new, where the old house had stood.

"Jeff!" said Dawn. "Come on. Give it a chance."

Jeff glowered at her, then turned to me, putting his hands on his hips. "What about the horse stalls? I bet they're gone. And the old feeding trough. All that stuff was so cool."

I agreed with him. "I know," I said. "That's why we saved a lot of it. The trough is out back, filled with flowers. It looks really nice. And we saved the brass nameplates from the horse stalls. Sharon thought you might want to put one up on the door of your room."

I saw that Jeff was interested in that idea, but he didn't crack a smile. "Did you save the one that said 'Captain'?" he asked.

"Yup."

"Well, I might want it," he said carelessly. "But it

won't make me feel any better about living in a stupid barn. I bet the whole place smells like hay and old spiderwebs."

Do old spiderwebs have a smell? I wasn't about to argue the point with Jeff. I knew what he meant. "Actually, it smells like fresh paint and — "

He interrupted. "What color did they paint my room?"

"We left that for you to decide," I answered, trying to ignore his challenging tone. "It's white right now, but you can choose any color you want."

"What if I want it to be — " Jeff paused, thinking — "black or orange or something?"

"It's your choice," I told him. "You're the one who will have to live with it." Sharon and I had discussed this very issue, knowing that a ten-year-old boy might pick the most disgusting color he could think of. We'd decided to let him do whatever he wanted. "Paint it orange *and* black if you want. Celebrate Halloween all year round."

Jeff still wouldn't smile. I gave up. "Let's go in," I said. "I can't wait to show you guys around."

Sunny had already disappeared inside with Sharon. I led Jeff and Dawn toward the big sliding doors that opened into the kitchen, thinking it would make an impression on them. "Cool, huh?" I asked as I shoved the doors along their tracks to expose the kitchen, with its fancy new appliances and butcher-block counters.

Dawn nodded, raising her eyebrows. "Not bad," she said.

"Dumb," Jeff mumbled. "Who ever heard of a kitchen with one whole wall missing?"

I let out a sigh. Just then, Sharon, my dad, and Sunny came into the kitchen. "This place is awesome!" Sunny pronounced. "Dawn, wait until you see your room. It's adorable."

Sharon smiled at Sunny. I did too. It was hard not to, when she was so enthusiastic. I could even feel Dawn softening. "Is that a new blender?" she asked, looking at the one on the counter. "It looks like it'll be good for making smoothies."

"It is," Sharon answered. "And I've stocked up on fruit and yogurt and soy milk. We can whip up a batch whenever you want."

"Yahoo!" Sunny cried. "I adore smoothies."

"I only like mango ones," Jeff said. "And they don't have fresh mangoes in Connecticut."

I saw Sharon and my dad exchange a glance. "Hey, pal," my dad said, "want to see your room?"

"I guess," Jeff answered grudgingly. He followed

my dad out of the kitchen, dragging his feet as if he needed to be towed along.

Sharon looked at me, eyebrows raised.

"He'll come around," I said. "He's just — "

"Surprised," Dawn finished. "So am I. I mean, I knew the plan. I knew you guys were going to renovate the barn. But even though we talked about it, I was never able to picture it. It's just so — so *different*."

"I love it," Sunny announced. "But I guess that's easy for me to say. I never even saw the house."

"The house was great," Dawn said softly.

"It was," Sharon agreed. "But this place is okay too. Want to see your room?"

"Sure," Dawn said. "Lead the way." She picked up her pack and followed Sharon, who gave a brief tour as we walked through the first floor.

"Dining room," she said, waving toward one end of the house. "Living room," she added, waving the other way.

Sunny laughed. "It's gorgeous. Can I stay forever?"

"I don't think your par — your dad would like that," Sharon said, catching herself before she said "parents."

I looked at Sunny to see if she'd noticed. She had.

I could see it in her face. Suddenly, the fact of Mrs. Winslow's death was right there among us.

I saw Dawn reach out and take Sunny's hand, just for one short moment. Their eyes met. Sunny gave Dawn a tiny half smile.

This all happened as we were climbing the stairs, and it filled the space of about three seconds, total. But it had a big impact on me. I could see that, just as I'd imagined, Sunny and Dawn were closer than ever. I couldn't help being glad for Sunny, that she had Dawn for a friend. She needed friends, and Dawn is a good one to have.

I also couldn't help the tiny jealous twinge I felt deep in my stomach.

But I tried to forget it as Sharon and I led Dawn to her room. Sharon opened the door, but before she could say anything, Sunny ran into the room, pulling Dawn along with her. Sunny's enthusiasm was back, full force. "Check it out!" she cried. "Look at that diamond-shaped window. Is that not the coolest thing you've ever seen?"

She bounced around the room, showing Dawn all its special features. "Look at the built-in bookcase," she said. "Isn't it perfect? I can just picture some of your dolphins there."

I had thought the same thing. I'd even pictured some of the dophins arrayed on top of the bookcase. But it was too late for me to say so. Sunny had beaten me to it.

Dawn stood in the middle of the room, turning slowly. "It's nice," she said. She stopped turning and looked directly at Sharon. "It really is," she added. "Thanks."

"It's not totally finished," Sharon rushed to say. "Those curtains are just temporary, until you find some you truly love. And I want you to pick out a bedspread too and a rug — just like Mary Anne did."

"Ooh, ooh!" Sunny jumped around like a kid waiting to be called on by her teacher. "I'll help! I'll help! I *love* picking out stuff like that."

"We can all go," Dawn agreed, looking at me. "I'd love to have help."

"Great," I said. "Maybe we can go to the mall soon?" I turned to check with Sharon.

"Sure. Absolutely," Sharon promised. She gave Dawn a quick hug. "Why don't you unpack a little? I'm going to go check on Jeff."

Sunny had already thrown her duffel on one of the twin beds. "I choose this one," she told Dawn after Sharon had left. "That okay?"

"Definitely." Dawn tossed her pack on the other bed. Then she unzipped it and started to pull out clothes and books. Sunny began to unpack her duffel too.

I felt a little awkward. "I guess I'll go," I said. "You guys have stuff to do." I watched for a second longer as Sunny pulled out a stack of old, worn-looking notebooks.

She held them up for Dawn to see. Raising her eyebrows, she cocked her head toward the bookshelf. "Okay?" she asked.

Dawn nodded. "Sure," she answered. "Of course."

Suddenly, I realized what the books were. They were Mrs. Winslow's diaries. I remembered Dawn telling me that Mrs. Winslow had given them to Sunny just before she died. They went all the way back to her school days. Sunny must really treasure them, I thought.

Once again, I felt that twinge. Sunny and Dawn were communicating in shorthand. They didn't have to speak in full sentences. That's what being best friends is about. I eased myself out of the room. "Well, see you," I said.

I heard them start to talk again as soon as I had

left. Were they talking about me, I wondered? Or were they talking about something else entirely, having forgotten all about me the second I wasn't there?

You know what's funny? I honestly didn't know which would be worse.

✳ Chapter 5

"It's going to be a scorcher, kiddies, so be cool and stay tuned to the hottest spot in Stoneybrook: WSTO, thirteen-thirteen on your dial!"

I snapped off the radio. I can't stand the morning DJ on WSTO. He's so loud and obnoxious. He does play good music, though, which is why I keep my radio turned to that station. Anyway, the only real alternative is EZ-Lite, the station my dad listens to. It plays all these dopey songs from when he was a teenager. Sometimes I'll catch him singing along with this goofy smile on his face. I love my dad, but I have to say it can be downright embarrassing to see him mouthing words to some "groovy" tune.

Anyway. Even though I can't stand Morning Mack (the DJ I'd just silenced), I had to admit he was probably right about the day's weather. I hadn't moved a muscle yet, unless you count flinging my arm toward the radio, and I was already hot. My new bedroom had felt pretty cool so far. But this morning it felt stuffy.

I sat up in bed and looked out the window. The sky outside was that milky white color that means it's going to be humid. "Ugh!" I said, flopping back onto my pillow. I can't stand that Triple H weather: Hot, Humid, and Hazy.

I heard giggling from down the hall. Dawn and Sunny must be awake too. I wondered what was so funny. Should I find out? Or would the giggling stop when I walked into the room? I rolled onto my back and put my pillow over my head. "Cut it out," I told myself. Sunny and Dawn were friends, and that was good. I didn't want to dwell on feeling left out.

In fact . . .

I jumped out of bed and pulled on a pair of shorts and a T-shirt. Then I headed for Dawn and Sunny's room and knocked lightly on the door. "It's me," I called.

"Come on in!" said Dawn.

"Good morning." Sunny rubbed her eyes and yawned as I walked into the room.

So much for feeling left out. I plopped down on Dawn's bed. "I heard you guys laughing," I said. "What's so funny?"

"Oh, I just had this silly dream," said Sunny. "I was telling Dawn about it." She glanced at Dawn and the two of them cracked up again. When she caught her breath, Sunny went on. "It was about this old teddy bear I once had. His name was Oogy. In my dream, I married him. I was wearing a white dress and everything. Dawn was one of my bridesmaids."

I giggled. "Hmmm," I said, stroking my chin. "Very interesting. And what do you think this means, Ms. Winslow?"

Sunny grinned. "I don't know, doctor," she said. "Do you think I have a strange fixation on stuffed animals?"

"We'll have to explore this further. Can you come three times a week from now on? And can you bring Mr. Oogy with you?"

Sunny threw a pillow at me, and we all cracked up.

Just then, there was a knock on the door. "Girls?" It was Sharon.

"Come on in, Mom," said Dawn. "We're up."

"I could hear *that* a mile away." Sharon smiled

around at us from the doorway. "So, I had an idea. How would you like to spend today at the pool? I could drop you off, and Richard could pick you up at the end of the day. It's going to be hot, hot, hot."

"Sounds excellent!" cried Sunny. "How soon do we have to be ready to go?"

Sharon checked her watch. "How does half an hour from now sound?"

"No problem!" Sunny bounced out of bed.

Sharon laughed. "Well, no problem for one of you," she said. "How about you two? Can you be ready?"

"Sure," said Dawn. "I'll just whip up some smoothies for our breakfast."

She'd apparently forgotten that I wasn't as crazy about smoothies as she was. "I'll have toast," I said. "But I guess I can be ready too."

"Great," said Sharon. "I'll be downstairs, then." She closed the door.

"Cool!" said Sunny. "The pool will be *the* place to be today. Won't it?"

I shrugged. "Probably," I said. I like the pool, but I don't necessarily love spending a whole day there. Still, it would be fun to go to the pool with Dawn and Sunny.

"You don't sound psyched," Sunny observed. She

looked at me closely. "Are you worried that Logan will be there?"

Whoa. I hadn't even thought of that. But as soon as she mentioned it, I *was* a little worried. I hadn't spent much time at the pool since Logan and I had broken up. What if he was there — with some other girl? Sunny was right. That could be awful. "I — I hadn't thought about it," I said.

"It'll be fine," said Dawn. "I doubt he'll be there." She jumped out of bed and started rummaging through her bureau drawers. "Now, where did I put my suit?" she muttered.

"I better find mine too," I said, getting up to head out the door.

"We're going to have a blast!" I heard Sunny say as I walked down the hall. "Are there usually cute guys at the pool? Maybe we can find one for Mary Anne."

Yikes. That was all I needed. Sunny as matchmaker. Then I thought of something and stopped short, right there outside my room. How did Sunny know that Logan and I had broken up anyway? Dawn must have told her. But how *much* had Dawn told her? Did Sunny know every detail of my personal life? I certainly didn't like that idea. Sure, I knew a little about what she'd gone through with her mother's illness. But I didn't want her knowing all kinds of private things about me.

I found my suit and threw it into a bag, along with a towel, a hat, some high-SPF sunscreen (I burn easily and never tan), a couple of magazines, and my water bottle. Ready or not, I was headed for the pool.

Sunny and Dawn were draining their smoothies when I walked into the kitchen. "Excellent!" Sunny said, finishing the last sip. "Super energy for a super day."

Did I think Sunny *needed* extra energy? Don't ask. But I had to smile at her. It was wonderful to see her acting so upbeat after everything she'd been through. Maybe this trip really would be good for her.

Fifteen minutes later, Sharon dropped us off at the pool. Jeff had come with us, but he immediately ran off to find the Pike boys and we barely saw him for the rest of the day. I think he spent most of his time in the Ping-Pong room.

Sunny took charge at the pool. "This looks like a good place," she said, staking out a spot for us by throwing down her towel. "Not too far from the refreshment stand, yet close to the lifeguard chair. That's where a lot of action goes on. At least, that's true at the beach." She gazed around. "Not many boys here yet," she said. "But it's early. I bet they'll show up when it gets hotter." She eyed me. "That suit looks great on you. Can you take that hat off, though? Your hair's so pretty."

I wasn't about to risk a sunburn by taking off my hat to impress boys. "Haven't you ever heard of skin cancer?" I said without thinking.

She stared at me. "I've heard of every kind of cancer," she replied quietly. "I've heard enough about cancer to last me a lifetime."

I felt about one inch tall. "Oh, Sunny," I said, "I'm so sorry. I really am. How could I say something like that?" I wanted to crawl under my towel. It's not like me to blurt out the wrong thing. That's Kristy's way, not mine. "I'm really, really sorry," I said again.

"No biggie," said Sunny, waving a hand. "I've heard it all before."

"But it must make you feel horrible when people mention cancer." Oh, no. I covered my mouth.

"Mary Anne," said Sunny impatiently, "don't worry about it. Really. It's no big deal. I'm not likely to forget that my mom died of cancer. So it's not as if you're reminding me of something I don't already know."

Dawn met my eyes and gave me a nod, as if to say, *Sunny's right. Don't worry.*

I didn't want to keep apologizing, so I gave it up. But I still felt terrible.

I guess that's why I went along with Sunny when she started flirting with Cole West — on my behalf.

Normally, I don't flirt with guys at the pool — or anywhere else. I'm just not the flirting type. But Sunny sure is. And she spotted Cole the second he walked out of the changing rooms.

"Ooh, he's cute," she said, following him with her eyes. "What do you think, Mary Anne?"

"I think he's a little old for you," I said. "He's in ninth grade." I knew who he was because he's on the high school junior varsity basketball team. Logan and I used to go to their games. Incidentally, I do think he's cute. Everybody does. He's tall, with black curly hair and dark brown eyes.

Sunny laughed. "First of all, a ninth-grader would be *young* for me, if anything," she said. "I happen to like older guys. And second of all, I asked what *you* think. You need a new boyfriend, and I think this dude looks like a good prospect." By then, she'd caught his eye. I saw her smile at him.

He smiled back.

Then he sauntered over to our towels.

"Whoa," I heard Dawn say under her breath. "Sunny's good, isn't she?"

I could hardly answer. She was so good it was scaring me. I could have spent every day for a month at the pool without a guy approaching me. But all Sunny had to do was smile and make eye contact. It was as if some force field were around her that drew guys in.

"Hey," said Cole, sitting down next to Sunny.

"Hey," Sunny replied. "What's up?"

"The sun." Cole grinned.

"Funny you should mention that. That's my name. Sunny."

"I'm Cole."

"And this is Dawn, and *this*," Sunny said, pausing significantly, "is Mary Anne." She gestured toward me as if I were some precious jewel she were showing off.

"I know you." Cole gave me a closer look. "Don't you go out with that guy Logan Bruno? He's a pretty good ballplayer."

"I used to," I said.

Cole nodded. "Cool."

Sunny gave me a Look.

Cole hung around for awhile. And by the time he left, he'd asked if the three of us wanted to go to a movie that weekend, with him and two of his friends. I would have hesitated, but Sunny? She said yes before I could say a word.

And I didn't want to put a damper on her enthusiasm. After all, she was here to heal and move on. If that meant I had to go to the movies with a bunch of boys I hardly knew, who was I to say no? I wanted Sunny to be happy.

❀ Chapter 6

At least on Tuesday I wanted Sunny to be happy. But by Friday I was beginning to wonder. A happy Sunny was, well, exhausting.

Sunny seemed to have endless energy. She woke up early and bounced out of bed with a smile. And she kept going full steam ahead until we all collapsed into bed at night. Sunny seemed to need to be in constant motion. She never sat still. She talked and laughed and kept Dawn and me — and Sharon and Richard and Jeff and everyone else who happened by — entertained.

On Wednesday Sunny made a humongous breakfast for our family, filling the kitchen with activity, piles of dirty dishes, and splotches of flour. Then she cleaned up just as fast, and began to clean the house as well. "I love to vacuum!" she insisted, grabbing the machine from Sharon and dashing around the downstairs with it. She plumped up couch pillows, straightened the dining room chairs, even scrubbed the bathroom sink.

"She's making us look bad," Dawn muttered to me at one point. "I think she's done more chores this morning than I've done in the last year!"

"Can't you make her stop?" I asked.

Dawn shook her head. "Once Sunny gets in this kind of mood, there's no stopping her."

"So what do we do?"

Dawn shrugged. "What's the old saying? If you can't beat them, join them? I guess we might as well follow her example."

After she'd cleaned the house from top to bottom (I'm exaggerating, but only barely), Sunny talked us into riding our bikes to the pool. That's a longer ride than I'm used to, and Dawn hadn't been riding much at all and felt out of shape, but Sunny insisted. She borrowed Jeff's bike, which was too small for her, and pedaled faster than either of us. We could barely keep her in sight.

Instead of spending her energy flirting with boys, Sunny decided we needed to practice diving. The

Stoneybrook pool complex has three pools: the Olympic-sized one we'd been sitting near the day before, a little wading pool for young kids, and a diving pool with three boards. One of the boards is low, one is mid-height, and one is scary-high.

Guess which one Sunny spent her time on?

She climbed up the ladder over and over. "Check this out!" she'd yell from the high board. Then she'd attempt a jackknife or a back flip. Some of them were pretty good. Sunny's had some experience and some lessons, I guess. I was impressed. But I wasn't tempted to join her. Dawn tried the high board a couple of times, then moved to the medium one. I stuck with the low board.

"Come on, chickens!" Sunny taunted us. "Those boards are for babies."

"Goo-goo," said Dawn, sticking her thumb in her mouth. "Then that's what I am."

"Me too," I said. Dawn seemed to understand how to handle Sunny's energy. You couldn't fight it; you just had to work around it.

I don't want to make it sound awful. In fact, watching Sunny zoom around was fun at times. And she certainly made things interesting. But keeping up with her wasn't easy.

On Thursday, after another huge breakfast,

Sunny asked Sharon if we could do some gardening for her. Naturally, Sharon was thrilled.

"Of course!" she said. "Come on outside and I'll show you what needs to be done."

While Sharon and Sunny toured the garden, Dawn and I finished cleaning up the kitchen. At first, we didn't say much. We just concentrated on clearing away dishes, putting pots into the sink, and wiping counters. Finally, I spoke up. "Sunny sure is — " I couldn't figure how to say it.

"Energetic? Peppy? Full of beans?" Dawn grinned at me. "I know. I'm kind of used to it, but I can tell she's tiring you out."

"It's fine," I said, waving a hand. "But isn't it just a little weird? I mean, because of her mom and all?"

I saw a shadow pass over Dawn's face. Sometimes I forgot how close she'd been to Mrs. Winslow. "I'm sorry, I — "

"No, it's okay. I know what you mean. I think it's just Sunny's way of coping." Dawn frowned down at the dish towel in her hand.

"Does she ever talk about — about her mom? Like, at night, when you guys are getting ready to sleep?"

Dawn shook her head. "Not really. We talk a lot but mostly about Ducky and Maggie and our other friends back home. Or about the boys at the pool, stuff like that. She never brings up her mom, so neither do I."

I nodded. "I understand." Sunny didn't exactly leave a lot of room for serious topics.

"I don't know if she's avoiding the subject," Dawn went on. Now she was folding and refolding the dish towel. "Or if she's just trying to rebuild her life — you know, move on."

"Well, whichever it is, I guess we just have to support her."

"Sure," said Dawn, brightening a bit. "As long as she doesn't force us off the high dive."

I laughed. "Nobody can do that. But I'm willing to put up with just about anything else."

"Me too." Dawn smiled. "Anyway, she's kind of fun when she's like this. Hanging out with Sunny can be like taking a ride on a roller coaster."

Just then, Sunny burst into the room. "You guys! Haven't you changed yet? We have a *ton* to do!"

Dawn and I looked at each other and smiled.

"Here's the plan," Sunny said, grabbing our hands to pull us upstairs. "First, we do some weeding. Then I'll mow the lawn while you guys clip around the edges. Then we can repot some of the geraniums Sharon kept from last summer and plant the seedlings she bought from the nursery."

"Sounds like a big day," said Dawn.

"Big day? That's only the morning!" Sunny laughed. "Wait until you hear about what we're doing this afternoon." She headed into Dawn's room to change.

Dawn hung back. "What do you think?" she whispered to me. "Are we going to dig our own swimming pool?"

We giggled. But by the end of the day, we weren't laughing. We were too tired to even crack a smile. Sunny had kept us on the run, with hardly a break for lunch or a rest in the shade.

As exhausted as I was, I had to admit the yard looked great when we were done. And Sharon couldn't have been happier.

"How about if I take you to the mall tomorrow as a reward?" she asked. "I think I can even afford to give you each a little spending money."

"Great!" Sunny accepted for all three of us. "Can we pick out the new curtains and stuff for Dawn's room?"

"Of course."

"Then I'm going to spend the evening with those

color swatches," Sunny said. "I love putting together cool combinations." She looked at me. "Your room could use a little more personality too," she added. "Want to look at the books with me?"

I shook my head. "I'm too tired. A bath and bed are all I want right now." I was hurt by her comment about my room, but I tried to hide that. I didn't want to make her feel bad.

Sunny shrugged. "No prob. I'll come up with some ideas, and you can see what you think."

Sunny must have stayed up until at least midnight looking over the color swatches. But guess who was raring to go first thing in the morning? "Time to get malled," she sang, banging on my door at eight o'clock.

"Sunny." I groaned. "The stores don't even open until ten."

"And we want to be there on the dot," she answered without a pause. "If there are any sales, we don't want to miss out on the good stuff, do we?"

I groaned again, this time under my breath. "Support her, support her," I whispered to myself. "Okay!" I called back, trying to sound enthusiastic. "I'll be up in a minute."

"I'll have breakfast ready by the time you're dressed," she answered. "Be there or be square."

Being square didn't sound so bad if it meant a few extra minutes in bed. But I knew I didn't really have a choice. I heaved myself out of bed and prepared for another Sunny day.

Over breakfast, Sunny showed us some of her decorating ideas, illustrating them with the swatches. I had to admit that she had a good sense of color and style. Her mom had been an artist, and it must have rubbed off on Sunny. She'd come up with a Mediterranean palette for Dawn — yellows, purples, and reds blending to create a colorful but coordinated look. She'd thought of some ideas for my room too. "I didn't mean to offend you when I said your room needed more personality," she said, giving me a sheepish smile. "But just look at how a little bit of this green would complete your color scheme."

I had to give Sunny credit for two things: one, for noticing that I'd been hurt by her comment, and two, for being right about the green. Suddenly, I was eager to head for the mall. If Sunny could help me find a pillow or two to complete my room, we'd both be happy.

So, how did our shopping trip go? Well, to make a long story short, I did find my pillows. But it took all day, and I didn't exactly have a lot of energy left over for my Friday night sitting job at the Pikes'.

Let's just say that "Sunny at the Mall" is not a show I need to repeat anytime soon. Not that it wasn't fun. It was. It was just a little too *much* fun for one day.

Sunny insisted on stopping into just about every store at the mall, since she wanted to have the total experience. We looked through the magazines at Bookcenter, tried on platform sandals at Antoinette's Shoe Tree, petted all the puppies at Critters, and listened to dozens of music samples on the headphones at Power Records. We even tried on veils at Rita's Bridal Shoppe.

By five o'clock my feet hurt. My eyes hurt. And my stomach hurt. (Could it have been that last round of nachos at Tortilla Queen?) But I had my pillows and Dawn had her curtains and bedspread, and, best of all, Sunny was happy.

❊ Chapter 7

"You look tired," Sharon said when she picked me up at the mall's side entrance.

"I am." I leaned back in my seat. "Wake me when we get to the Pikes'." I was just kidding, but in truth I could have used a nap. Sunny and Dawn were lucky. They were going to a movie. If they wanted to, they could doze right through the whole thing. Not that it would be easy; they'd chosen a scary one about zombies terrorizing a summer camp. I was glad to miss it — but once again, I couldn't help feeling a little left out.

It was silly. I should have been happy. I was on my way to a sitting job (and I do love baby-sitting), and I'd be sharing that job with my other best friend, Kristy (Mallory was away at a two-week writing camp). So why did I care that Dawn and Sunny hardly seemed to notice when I said good-bye? They already had their minds on popcorn and zombies. It wasn't anything personal.

"What movie are they going to?" Jeff asked from the backseat. I'd barely noticed he was there, since he was slumped way down.

"*Camp Fear*," I told him.

"Cool," he said. "I wish I could go."

"No way," Sharon told him.

"I know, I know." Jeff groaned. "I'm too young, too impressionable. I'll have nightmares."

"You've got it, buddy." Sharon and I smiled at each other. "Anyway," she went on, "you have plans tonight. The triplets are excited about having you over."

I'd asked Mr. and Mrs. Pike if it was okay to bring Jeff along when I sat. I was a little concerned about him, and I knew Sharon and my dad were too. He was still in a funk about the house. He hadn't done a thing about decorating his room or making it his own. We'd all offered to help. Sunny had even sketched out a very cool idea for a big *Star Wars* mural to go on the wall over his bed. But Jeff didn't seem interested. I figured it might do him good to spend some time with his friends.

When we arrived at the Pikes', Kristy was already there and Mr. and Mrs. Pike were on their way out the door. "Hi, Mary Anne, 'bye Mary Anne!" said Mrs. Pike. "Good to see you, Jeff. Have fun!"

Jeff headed off downstairs to the Pikes' rec room.

"Boy, do you look tired." That was the first thing Kristy said to me. "Did you have fun at the mall?"

I was about to start telling her about our day when Jordan interrupted. Jordan's ten, like his brothers Adam and Byron. They're the triplets, obviously. "When's dinner?" he demanded.

"Any minute now," Kristy said, checking her watch. "I'm just waiting for the frogs to spawn. I already put the monkey-brain pie into the oven. And dessert's all set: The booger pudding is in the fridge."

"Eww!" Jordan cried gleefully. "I'm going to hurl!" Kristy knows just what ten-year-old boys like to hear. "Hey, guys!" Jordan took off down the hall. "Wait till you hear what's for dinner!"

A few beats later, we heard loud (fake) barfing noises from the rec room. Kristy and I grinned at each other.

"What are we really having?" I asked.

"Macaroni and cheese, broccoli, and ice-cream sandwiches," Kristy answered. "If anyone wants something different, they're welcome to rummage around in the fridge."

"Jeff likes mac and cheese. He'll be happy."

"Will he?" Kristy asked. "Judging by the way he looked coming in, it would take more than a good dinner to cheer him up. Is he still upset about the house?"

I nodded. "He — "

Just then, we were interrupted again. This time it was Claire, the youngest Pike. She's five. "Can you thread my needle?" she asked. "Margo and me are doing a crafts project. We're making purses."

"Margo and I," I said, automatically correcting her as I took the needle and began to thread it. (Margo is the next-youngest. She's seven.)

"Margo and you?" she asked, looking bewildered. "But you just got here."

"No — I — oh, never mind." I handed her back the needle. "You're all set," I said. "But don't go far. Dinner will be ready in a few minutes."

Claire thanked me and ran off.

"Where's Vanessa?" I asked.

"She's in her room," Kristy told me. "She's reading a biography of Emily Dickinson. Her mom said she's so deeply into it that she's barely spoken to anyone for two days."

Vanessa's nine. She loves poetry and hopes to be a poet someday.

Kristy and I headed for the kitchen and finished putting dinner together. I set the table and poured out glasses of milk while Kristy served the macaroni and cheese. Then we called the kids.

It took fifteen minutes to get everyone seated at the table — and about three and a half minutes for everyone to eat.

"May I be excused?" Adam asked after he'd rushed through his plate of food.

"No excuse for you," Jordan muttered.

"Jordan!" Vanessa said. "Think twice. Be nice."

I wondered if that's what Emily Dickinson would have said. As far as I remembered, her poetry didn't always rhyme. Vanessa's usually does.

"I'm done too," said Claire, hiding her last piece of broccoli under the rim of her plate.

"Almost," I said, pointing to it. "Finish that and then you can go back to your project."

Margo had already eaten all her broccoli. I think she's the only Pike kid who actually likes vegetables.

Adam and Byron stood up to take their plates to the sink. "Wait up, you guys!" said Nicky, shoving a last forkful of macaroni into his mouth. Nicky, who's eight, is always trailing along after the triplets.

Adam rolled his eyes.

Byron waited. He tends to be a little more thoughtful than his brothers.

I glanced at Jeff. He hadn't eaten much. Instead, he was playing with his food. He stuck a broccoli flower upright in a pile of macaroni so that it looked like a tree. Then he knocked it over as if he were Paul Bunyan.

"Timber!" I said under my breath. I gave him a private smile. He didn't smile back.

"What are you guys up to?" I asked him.

He shrugged.

"Having fun?"

He shrugged again.

Byron touched Jeff on the shoulder. "It's your turn on the computer," he said. "I can show you how to get around the evil wizard, if you want."

"That's okay," said Jeff. "Adam can take my turn. He's better at it anyway."

"Cool!" yelled Adam. He ran to the sink, dumped his plate, and reappeared carrying an ice-cream sandwich.

"Better eat that outside," Kristy advised. "I don't think your dad would appreciate ice cream on the computer."

Adam made a face, then headed out the back door, letting the screen door slam. Jordan and Nicky followed in his tracks, each with his own ice-cream sandwich. Byron watched them go, then looked back at Jeff.

"Go ahead," Jeff told him. "I don't think I want any ice cream anyway. I'll catch up with you guys."

Poor Jeff. Even Claire noticed that something was wrong. "Want to come sew with us?" she asked, flashing him her best smile.

"No, thanks," Jeff said.

Claire and Margo ran off, and Vanessa disappeared upstairs to commune with Emily. Kristy and I puttered around the kitchen, cleaning up. Jeff continued to sit at the empty table.

"Don't you want to play with your friends?" I asked him.

He shook his head. He wouldn't look at me.

"Jeff? Are you okay?"

He burst into tears.

"Oh, Jeff!" I was surprised. It took a *lot* to make him cry. "What's the matter?"

For a few moments, he couldn't talk. He cried and cried. I sat down next to him and tried to comfort him. Then his sobs died down a little. I motioned for Kristy to leave us alone.

"Jeff, can you talk to me?" I asked. "Tell me what's wrong."

"I just — I just hate it here. I hate Connecticut. There's nothing here I like." He sniffed. "I used to like our house, but now — now it's gone!" he wailed. "And I used to like to play in the barn, but now I have to *live* in the barn. And I don't have any of my stuff, and everybody keeps telling me to get *new* stuff, but it'll never be the same as the stuff that got burned up. I miss my stuff!"

I nodded. I missed my "stuff" too. I rubbed his back. "I know, Jeff. It's hard."

"And my friends don't understand, and I feel like I don't even know them anymore." Jeff hiccuped.

I knew how *that* felt too. My friends had been supportive and incredibly thoughtful, but none of them really understood what it had been like to lose everything in a fire. How could they? But I knew they'd tried, and I knew the Pike boys had too. "Jeff," I said. "Your friends want to help. They want to understand. And they want things to be the same between you."

"But they aren't!" Jeff cried. "Nothing's the same since that stupid, stupid fire."

He was right. I couldn't deny it. And while I'd had lots of time to work through my feelings about the fire, Jeff was having a delayed reaction. The fact that his home had been lost was just starting to hit him, even though it had happened months ago.

Just then, I turned to see Byron standing quietly in the doorway. He looked sympathetic. Suddenly, I had an idea. "Hey, Jeff," I said. "You know what? I bet your friends would love to help you figure out how to fix up your room so you're happier in it."

"No, they wouldn't," Jeff mumbled.

"Oh, yeah?" Byron asked from the doorway. "Yes, we would. That would be cool!"

Good old Byron. I smiled at him.

Jeff looked up. "Really?" he asked.

"Wait here," said Byron. "I'll get the others." He dashed off and rounded up the rest of the Pike boys. Within minutes, everyone was sitting around the dining room table, plotting and planning.

Did I say Sunny was a good interior decorator? Well, she had nothing on the Pike boys. They came up with some outrageously creative ideas.

"I have this real cool monster mask," Jordan said. "We could make a scarecrow with it and stand it in the corner. It would scare everybody to death!"

"And we can paint the room purple," added Adam. "With red racing stripes around it. And put up black-light posters and keep the black light on all the time."

"You can have my Nerf basketball net," Nicky offered generously.

"Or even our real basketball net!" cried Byron, getting carried away.

Kristy had come in by then, and she and I looked at each other and smiled. I'm sure she was thinking the same thing I was: that Sharon and Dad might not be so pleased with the new decorating team I'd hired. On the other hand, if it made Jeff feel better about the new house, they'd probably let him keep an orangutan in his room.

❋ Chapter 8

"What about a bed that looks like an aircraft carrier? Do they make those? That would be *really* cool."

"Jeff," Dawn said. She sounded exasperated. "Enough, okay? I know you're excited about changing your room around, but we have stuff to do now. We'll help out when your friends come over tomorrow, I promise."

It was Saturday evening, the day after my sitting job at the Pikes'. Jeff had been talking all day about the plans he and the triplets and Nicky had made for fixing up his room. He could hardly wait. Sunny had encouraged him, naturally, showing him outrageous color combinations and discussing what kind of live animal habitats might be fun (I actually heard them talking about an iguana house at one point). But even though we were happy to see Jeff acting less mopey, Dawn and I were already tired of the subject.

Anyway, Dawn was right. We *did* have other stuff to do.

We had to get ready for our date.

Gulp.

Just *thinking* the word made me nervous.

I hadn't been on a date with anybody but Logan in a long, long time. And going out with Logan had been so easy, so comfortable. I never had to think about what to say or how to act around him.

I never had to think about what to wear.

"What about this?" I held up a purple T-shirt. Dawn and I were alone in her room, now that Jeff had finally left. Sunny was downstairs, talking to her dad on the phone. We'd thrown piles of clothes — mine, hers, and Sunny's — on both beds, and we were starting to try them on, deciding what to wear that night when we went to the movies with Cole and his friends.

"With what?" asked Dawn, considering the shirt. "Your denim skirt?"

"I was thinking khakis," I admitted. "I don't want to feel overdressed."

"The skirt's not dressy."

"I know. It's just that — I haven't been on a *date* date in so long. I don't want it to be a big deal." I threw down the T-shirt and picked up a black tank top of Sunny's. I put that right down. It was *so* not me.

"First of all," Dawn told me, "it's *not* a *date* date. It's just a bunch of kids going to the movies together. And it's not a big deal. So what you wear really doesn't matter at all."

I picked up another T-shirt, a green one with blue stripes. "You're probably right." I sighed. "I guess I'm just nervous. And I'm not really sure I'm ready for this. You know, the dating thing." I saw Dawn open her mouth, and I rushed to correct myself. "I mean, the 'bunch of kids going to the movies together' thing."

Dawn laughed. "You'll be fine. Just do what Mom always says to do."

"Be yourself," we chorused. We were still laughing when Sunny walked in.

"Hey, what's the joke?" she asked.

"Nothing, really," I said.

"Mary Anne's a little nervous about tonight, so I'm just trying to take her mind off it," Dawn explained.

"Nervous?" Sunny repeated. "Come on, Mary Anne, get a clue. You have *nada* to be nervous about. Cole is *nuts* about you. I predict that this is only the first of many, many excellent dates."

There was that word. "I knew it!" I said, throwing the T-shirt I was holding at Dawn. "It *is* a date. It *is*."

Dawn threw the T-shirt at Sunny. "See what you've done? I almost had her all calmed down."

Sunny grinned and shrugged. "Oh, well. Calm is overrated anyway. Let's figure out what we're going to wear!" She started grabbing at clothes, flinging them left and right as she dug through the piles. "Whose skirt is this? It's adorable! Can I wear it? Can I have it? What goes with it?"

Dawn and I exchanged a glance. Sunny was in high gear and there was no stopping her now. We might as well join in.

"It's mine," I said. "You can wear it, but you can't have it, and it goes with just about anything. Try this." I tossed her black tank top over.

Sunny pulled on the skirt and tank and danced around for a second in front of the full-length mirror on the closet door. "Da-da-da-da," she sang under her breath. Then she stopped moving.

"Nope!" She turned back to the piles of clothes.

Dawn and I settled on our outfits pretty quickly (me: khakis and a white shirt, Dawn: long skirt, tank top) but Sunny was trying on clothes well after Sharon's fifteen-minute warning (Sharon was driving us to the mall to meet Cole and his friends). In fact, Sunny was still putting herself together as we drove to the mall. She applied lip gloss, tried on four pairs of earrings, and even changed her shoes (she'd brought along three pairs, just in case).

I honestly didn't mind Sunny's energy. It took my mind off my own uncertainty. But I could see that Dawn was losing patience. I'd asked her about it earlier. "I know it's exhausting, but she seems happy," I said.

"*Seems* is the right word," Dawn said. "Don't get me wrong. I'm glad she's not sitting around crying, but sometimes I think this is just a surface thing. You know — as long as she *acts* as if everything's wonderful, it will be. And if she keeps busy enough, she won't have to think. But I know there's a lot of pain underneath it all. When is that going to come out?"

I patted Dawn on the shoulder. I knew she wasn't looking for a real answer. She was just worried about

Sunny. And I could understand that. Still, we were doing all we could. We couldn't *make* her deal with her pain.

Sunny joined us then, wearing my skirt paired with a white baby-T, and we piled into Sharon's car. A little while later, we were piling out — in front of Cole and his friends, who were waiting at the main entrance to the mall.

"Hey," said Cole. He shook his hair out of his eyes and smiled right at me. I couldn't deny that he was very, very cute.

"Hi," I said, looking down at my shoes. That's a terrible habit of mine: I've been doing it as long as I can remember.

Cole's friends were hanging back a little. One was blond with freckles, and the other had brown hair and — I hate to say it — a whole bunch of pimples on his face.

"This is Jason," Cole said, waving a hand at the blond boy, "and that's Alex."

"Hey," said Alex, looking down at his feet.

At least I wasn't the only one.

"Hi," said Jason. He was staring at Sunny, and I saw his cheeks turn pink. Poor guy. He was blushing.

"Shall we?" asked Cole, giving me a mock bow. I

had to admit he was a lot smoother than most of the boys I know. Was that because he was older? Or was it just his personality?

"Um, sure," I said. He opened the door for me and we walked inside with the others following.

"You look nice," Cole told me as we stood in line for our tickets.

"Um, thanks." Behind us, I heard Jason and Alex talking about a video game. And behind *them*, Sunny and Dawn were giggling about something.

I had a feeling this night was going to seem very long.

The movie was okay. After a little indecisiveness, we'd settled on one about a family that gets marooned on a desert island. The only thing I didn't like was that when we sat down, after stocking up on popcorn, soda, and jelly beans, Cole arranged things so that he was sitting next to me. Alex was on my other side, then Sunny, then Jason, then Dawn. So it was boy-girl-boy-girl.

I'd definitely have preferred to sit between Sunny and Dawn.

The good thing? Cole did not try to hold my hand or kiss me. He did lean over and whisper into my ear a couple of times, asking if I knew who a certain actress was or pointing to something on the screen. But that didn't bother me. Too much.

Afterward, we headed back to Stoneybrook by bus and landed at the Rosebud for milk shakes. I was worried that I might see Logan, since he works there as a busboy now and then, but fortunately he was nowhere in sight.

Sunny was still "on." She kept talking about how cool the movie had been and how she wished *she* could be marooned on a desert island. "Only not with my family, if you know what I mean," she said to Jason, giving him a flirtatious look.

Jason blushed.

"Don't you think it would be romantic?" she went on. "You know, the full moon, an empty island, the crashing surf . . ." She looked dreamy.

Jason blushed even redder.

I saw Dawn nudge Sunny under the table, and I knew just what that meant. It meant, *Sunny, leave the poor guy alone!*

Sunny knew it too. But she couldn't seem to stop. She flirted with Jason until I thought he was going to turn the color of a fire engine. And every time Dawn nudged her, she just cranked it up a notch.

I wanted to crawl under the table.

"What's the matter?" Cole asked me, looking concerned.

"Nothing," I said. I took a sip of my shake.

"Is it me?" he asked quietly. "You don't like me, do you?"

Yikes. "No — I mean, yes, I mean — no, it's really not about you." I tried to reassure him. I certainly didn't *dis*like him. He was nice enough, and considerate and funny. But he wasn't my type. He was a little too cocky, a little too sure of himself.

Try to tell that to Sunny, though. When we were finally home, going over the evening while we lay around in Dawn and Sunny's room, she would not stop raving about Cole.

"He is so cool," she said. "You and he look *adorable* together. You're going to be an awesome couple. Don't you think?" She turned to Dawn.

"Sure." Dawn shrugged. Then she yawned.

"You're not *tired*, are you?" Sunny stared at Dawn. "I thought we could go outside. There's a full moon tonight, you know. I love to walk around in the moonlight. Everything looks so silvery."

Her enthusiasm was almost contagious. If I hadn't been exhausted, I might have gone outside with her. But it was nearly midnight by then. I was just too tired, and so was Dawn.

Sunny sulked a little. "You guys are no fun," she said, plopping herself down on her bed. Then I saw her yawn. Finally! She was tired too. I tiptoed down the hall to my room and fell into my bed, exhausted. How was I going to stand an entire month of Sunny days?

❀ Chapter 9

It's not that I don't appreciate your help —
I like Cole, I just don't like like him, you know?
Sunny, I don't know how to tell you this, but —

I lay in bed the next morning, trying to figure out how to let Sunny know that Cole and I were not destined to be the next Romeo and Juliet, or even the next Homer and Marge Simpson. In fact, we weren't meant to be a couple at all. He was definitely not my type, and I sure wasn't his, whether he knew it or not.

But I knew Sunny would be disappointed. She'd put some effort into bringing us together, and nothing would make her happier than to see her matchmaking work out. It was important to me to keep Sunny happy — but I wasn't about to go out with some boy I didn't feel anything for just to cheer up a friend.

I nodded. *That's right*, I told myself. *Be strong. If Sunny likes him so much, maybe she should go out with him.*

It wasn't like me to be so assertive. But I didn't have much choice. Sunny was like a steamroller, and if I didn't get myself out of her path, I just might find myself walking up the aisle with Cole to the tune of "Here Comes the Bride."

I rolled out of bed and pulled on my bathrobe. Then I marched down the hall to Dawn's room and tapped on the door. "Are you guys up yet?" I called softly.

"Come on in," Dawn called back.

I pushed open the door and walked in. Sunny and Dawn were awake, but both of them were still lounging in bed. I sat down in Dawn's purple inflatable chair (one of the furnishings Sunny had talked her into). "Hey, Mary Anne!" Sunny cried. "We were just talking about you and Cole."

Gulp.

"Right," I began. "About that — "

"He is *so* not right for you," Sunny rushed on. "I thought he was at first, but now I can tell he's not."

My mouth was hanging open. "What — "

"I know it might be hard to cut him loose, especially since he's so nuts about you," she went on. Now she was sitting up in bed, braiding her hair while she talked. "I know how you are about hurting people's feelings. But we'll figure out some way for you to let him down easy."

"Sunny, I — "

Dawn laughed. "Forget it, Mary Anne. No matter what you think, Sunny's made up her mind."

"Where are those purple hair ties I bought the other day?" Sunny asked, holding one of her braids. "Oh, they're on the dresser. Can you toss me one, Mary Anne?"

I stood up, found the hair ties, and brought her one. "Thanks," she said. "So, anyway. You'll dump Cole."

Dump Cole? Did she have to put it that way? My face must have shown how I felt.

"Okay, okay, you don't have to *dump* him. But we won't be going out with that bunch of losers anymore."

"Sunny!" Now Dawn looked upset.

"Oh, come on. Did you see the zits on that guy's face?"

Dawn frowned. "Don't be mean, Sunny. What would Ducky think if he heard you talking like that?"

Sunny suddenly lost her grin. "Okay, you're right," she said quietly.

Wow. I knew Ducky, this boy out in California, was a good friend to Sunny and Dawn. But I didn't know his opinion was that important. I was glad there was someone Sunny cared about pleasing.

"So they're not losers," she went on. "Fine. Whatever. But still, we're not going out with them again. Okay with both of you?"

"Definitely," I said, sighing with relief.

"Okay," said Dawn. "But I did think Alex was kind of cute."

"Sure, if you like guinea pigs," Sunny mumbled under her breath.

I almost laughed, thinking of Alex's plump cheeks.

"What?" asked Dawn.

"Nothing! I didn't say a thing!" Sunny held up her hands.

"That's good," said Dawn. "Because I don't want to have to tell Ducky you did."

"Okay, okay." Sunny rolled her eyes. "Anyway,

those guys are so yesterday. It's time for us to move on."

"Move on?" I asked. "Do we have to?"

Sunny nodded. "Absolutely. What you need, I've decided, is an older guy."

I felt a chill run down my spine. Had I heard her correctly? "What?" I asked, hoping I hadn't.

"An older guy. Someone more mature. More exciting. More — *experienced*." Sunny gave that last word special emphasis.

"Oh, no," I said, shaking my head. "That's not what I need at all."

"Sure you do," said Sunny. "Believe me, there's nothing like an older guy. They are *so* romantic, and so much cooler than guys our age. Like this guy Carson I was seeing for awhile. He was older, and he was so awesome." She stared off into space. "We met at the beach," she said dreamily. "He had traveled all over, and he introduced me to some incredible books and ideas." Her eyes were closed now, and she smiled to herself.

"Carson?" Dawn asked incredulously. "You're not saying that he would have made a good boyfriend for Mary Anne, are you?"

I had a feeling there was more to the Carson story than Sunny was telling me.

Sunny opened her eyes. "Of course not!" she exclaimed. "But someone *like* him. Maybe a city guy. Doesn't your friend Stacey have a boyfriend who lives in the city? I bet he's way more sophisticated than these Connecticut guys."

I had to admit she was probably right about that. Ethan, this boy that Stacey has gone out with off and on, is an artist. He's very cool. Still. "Sunny — " I began. I wanted to explain that sophistication was not exactly what I was looking for. That, in fact, I wasn't looking for a boyfriend at all.

"Don't thank me," Sunny said, raising a hand. "And don't worry about a thing. I know just what you want, and I intend to find him for you before I go back home. That's my fondest wish, to see you with a terrific new boyfriend."

I slumped back in my chair. What could I say? Sunny had an agenda. "Well, I'm going to go get dressed," I said finally. "I'll see you guys downstairs."

As I left their room, I heard footsteps downstairs. *Lots* of footsteps. In fact, it sounded like a herd of buffalo. What was going on? Then I heard voices. "Yo, Jeff! Time to wake up!"

Oh, no! It was the Pike boys. They'd come over to help Jeff with his room — and there I was, walking down the hall in my bathrobe and pj's. They hit the stairs before I could make a dash for my room.

"Mary Anne!" said Byron, stopping in his tracks. I saw his cheeks turn red.

Mine felt hot, and I knew I was blushing too. I don't know which of us was more embarrassed. "Hi, Byron," I said, trying to sound casual. After all, he has sisters. He's seen girls in their bathrobes before.

"Hey, Mary Anne!" said Jordan from behind him. "Woo, woo, nice robe!"

Jordan doesn't embarrass as easily as some boys. Neither does Adam. He grinned at me. And Nicky? He's too young for it to matter.

I edged past the boys. "Jeff's room is that way," I said, pointing. "He's probably not up yet."

"He will be soon!" Jordan ran down the hall and started banging on Jeff's door. "The decorating squad is here!" he yelled.

I sighed. I'd almost forgotten about the day's project: Operation Jeff's Room.

"Um, see you," said Byron, backing his way down the hall to join the other boys, who were knocking on Jeff's door by then.

"Right," I said. I backed into my own room and closed the door behind me. I wished I could just hide in there for awhile. At least until Jeff's room was done, if not until Sunny had gone back to California.

But guess what. It turned out to be a fun day. For one thing, Sunny was focused on something other than finding me a boyfriend. And for another, well, let's just say it's pretty entertaining to watch five grade-school boys turn into interior decorators.

Over breakfast, the Pike boys and Jeff discussed ideas. Byron took notes:

IDEAS FOR JEFF'S ROOM

— Space station
— Dinosaur world — jungel with
    vines to climb
— Gorey bloody stuff (hands,
    scary faces, ect.)
— Basketball theem
— Surf shack (sunnie's idea)

At first Jeff especially liked the surf shack idea, since it would remind him of California. Adam was pushing hard for the "gorey bloody" theme, while Jordan wanted to create a *Lost World* effect, complete with animated dinosaurs. Byron liked the space station idea.

For awhile, the boys argued back and forth at

full volume. Dawn and I watched and listened. Sunny jumped in with her own two cents.

Then, grabbing a moment when all four older boys happened to have their mouths full of whole-wheat pancakes, Nicky spoke up. "What about a superhero theme?" he asked. "Don't you already have a bunch of action figures and stuff? We could make your room into a kind of headquarters for those guys. Like a clubhouse where they all hang out."

"Dumb, dumb, dumb," said Adam automatically.

"Wait a minute," Sunny said. "Think about it." She grabbed another piece of paper and started to make a list. "Tell me what superhero stuff you already have," she said to Jeff.

It turned out that he had a lot. He had plenty of action figures, as Nicky had pointed out. Plus he had X-Men sheets, an Incredible Hulk Halloween costume, a Batmobile, and a Batcave.

"We're on our way," cried Sunny. "This is it!"

Her enthusiasm was infectious. The boys flew into action, and by the end of the afternoon, Jeff's room had been transformed — without anyone's spending a penny.

It really did look like a clubhouse by the time Sunny had finished a sign for the door. Action figures stood all around in various poses. The X-Men sheets had been made into curtains. The Incredible Hulk costume was standing in a corner, guarding the Batcave. And a huge, complicated spiderweb, made out of string, was hanging from the ceiling with a Spiderman action figure in the center.

The best part was, as Jeff had said, that it didn't have to be permanent, especially since it hadn't cost anything. If he got tired of it, he could try out one of the other ideas they'd come up with. But for now, he was happy.

❀ Chapter 10

"Wow! All my favorites!" Jeff's eyes lit up when he saw the spread on the dining room table that night.

"It's to celebrate your new room," Sharon said, beaming. "You did a great job, honey. So Richard and I wanted to make you a special dinner."

Jeff grinned. "Yum," he said, looking over the food.

Yum was right. Sharon and my dad had created a feast. There was a huge pan of vegetarian lasagna, a basket of garlic bread, and a Caesar salad with homemade croutons (my dad's specialty). There were also meatballs made with seitan, which is a vegetarian alternative to meat (believe it or not, it can actually taste good), and a pitcher of iced tea.

"Make sure to save room for dessert," Sharon

told us. "I made carob brownies, and Richard brought home ice cream to put on top of them. There's even Tofutti for those of us who prefer it," she added, winking at Dawn. (Tofutti is ice cream made out of — gag me — tofu. Dawn and Sharon love it.)

"Yahoo!" cried Jeff.

"All right!" echoed Sunny. "Tofutti rules."

I should have known.

"Who doesn't love brownies à la mode?" asked my dad. "But right now I'm ready for some lasagna. Pass your plates, everybody, and I'll serve it."

For awhile, everyone was busy loading up their plates with food. Then there was a long period when nobody talked at all; we were too busy eating. Finally, Jeff spoke up.

"This is the best dinner ever," he said.

"I'm glad you like it." Sharon beamed.

Dawn giggled. "Hey, Jeff, the sauce on this reminds me. Remember that time we tried to make spaghetti sauce in the pressure cooker? We didn't have a clue about how to use that thing."

Jeff burst out laughing. "Mom thought there'd been some kind of terrible accident in the kitchen," he said. "She actually screamed when she first came in."

"Who could blame me?" Sharon asked. "Everything was covered in red. The walls were dripping. The cabinets were full of sauce. Even the ceiling was spattered. It looked like a scene from a horror movie."

"It was the first time we'd tried to make dinner on our own," Dawn told Sunny and me. "We wanted to surprise Mom. It was her birthday or something."

"No, it was Mother's Day!" said Jeff, remembering.

"We ended up going out for burritos." Dawn helped herself to another serving of salad. "We didn't even clean the kitchen first. We just left it and headed out. It was *such* a mess."

"But, being the well-behaved children that you are, I'm sure you cleaned up when you got home," put in my dad, with a grin.

"Um, right!" said Jeff. "I mean, we must have. Didn't we?"

Sharon just smiled.

"You kids have made some good meals since then," my dad said. "Mary Anne, do you remember the welcome-home dinner you and Dawn made me when I was coming back from that business trip?"

"I remember!" cried Dawn. "That was when I was trying to convince you to be a vegetarian. We made great stuff. A zucchini casserole, ginger-garlic tofu, a huge salad . . ."

"And I loved every bite." My dad smiled. "Because my girls made it for me."

Jeff made a gagging noise. "Goop alert! Goop alert!" he said, rolling his eyes. He can't stand it when people get sentimental.

We laughed. I looked around the table at all the happy faces. Then I took another look at one of them. Sunny's. She was laughing, just like the rest of us. But something was missing.

Something I recognized.

Something most people probably wouldn't have noticed.

But I did, because I knew exactly how she felt.

There we were, one big happy family, reliving happy memories. Talking, laughing, passing dishes of food. It was a nice scene. And to most people Sunny would have looked like a part of it, like she was having just as good a time as the rest of us. But I knew better.

We'd done everything we could to make Sunny feel at home, to make her feel welcome. Yet I saw that she still felt like an outsider, like a spectator at the happy-family parade.

I'd felt that way so often over the years. Sometimes I *still* feel that way. I mean, I have a family. And — don't get me wrong — I love my family a lot. I value the people in it above anything else. But I grew up without a mother, and I always feel that she's missing. Most people seem to take family for granted, as if it's like the air you breathe or the water you drink. But I know better. And now, so does Sunny.

Sunny looked up from her plate and caught me studying her. Our eyes met for just a second, and I saw the pain in hers. Then she looked away. "Hey, Dawn," she said. "What about that cake we made for your dad's birthday? When we used salt instead of sugar by mistake?"

Jeff groaned. "That had to be the worst cake in the history of the universe."

"Speaking of cake," Sharon said, "isn't it about time for dessert?"

The brownies were excellent. We piled on the ice cream (or Tofutti, depending), and by the time we left the table, everybody was moaning about being way too full. Even Jeff hadn't been able to handle seconds on dessert.

After dinner, Jeff headed upstairs to his new

room. Dawn, Dad, Sharon, and I hung out in the living room while Sunny put in a Sunday evening call to her dad. She was using the phone in Sharon and my dad's room. The call must not have lasted long, because after a few minutes I heard her footsteps padding down the hall to Dawn's room. She didn't come downstairs.

I couldn't stop thinking about the look I'd seen on her face, the "I don't belong" look. And I couldn't help wondering if she might want to talk about it. I wanted her to know I was willing to listen.

I yawned. "I'm kind of tired," I told the others. "I think I'll go up to my room and read for awhile." I kissed my dad and Sharon. "Thanks again for a great dinner," I told them.

Upstairs, I approached the closed door to Dawn's room. I knocked gently. "Sunny, it's me, Mary Anne," I said, pushing the door open. "How's your dad?"

"Fine, I guess," she said. She was lying on her bed, staring at the ceiling. "I mean, I don't know. He misses me, and he's all alone in that house. Sometimes I wonder if I should go back there."

"I'm sure he does miss you. But he understands that you want to be here with Dawn too."

"I know. And he's so busy at the bookstore that I'd probably never see him anyway."

I sat down on Dawn's bed. "Um, Sunny," I said, not knowing exactly where to start, "I was wondering, I mean, I just wanted you to know — "

She interrupted. "Mary Anne, do I have to call Jeff in here for a goop alert?" She rolled over on her side, facing me.

"No! I mean, I don't mean to be goopy. I just thought you might want to talk, you know, about — "

"I don't want to talk about anything," Sunny said firmly.

"I know it's hard," I went on. "Like at dinner. I know how that can be, watching everybody else be this happy family."

Sunny closed her eyes for a moment. Then she opened them and looked at me. "Was that not a riot, about the spaghetti sauce all over the kitchen?" she asked, grinning.

Okay. The message could not have been more clear. Sunny didn't want to talk. And whether I thought she should was beside the point. I couldn't force her to deal with her feelings. I couldn't demand that she open up about how her mother's death had affected her. And, the truth was, even though I thought I understood, I probably didn't. Her situation was so different from mine. I had no right to push her into anything she wasn't ready for.

"It was pretty funny," I agreed. I stood up and yawned. "Well, I guess I'll head to bed."

That was it. I figured Sunny would let me know when she was ready to talk. Meanwhile, I became her supportive friend again. And Sunny continued to be Ms. Energy Source of the Year.

Dawn had been absolutely right.

It wasn't just that Sunny didn't want to talk.

Sunny didn't want to think.

That seemed to be her solution: If she could just stay busy enough, she wouldn't have to face her thoughts. And if Sunny was going to be busy, so were Dawn and I, like it or not.

We spent the next three days in constant motion. Sunny led us from the pool to the mall to downtown to the library.

"And let's go to the arboretum. And the Stoneybrook Museum. I've already been to the library, but I still want to go back there. And what about the radio station? Could we go there? I bet they'd show us around."

Finally, by Wednesday night, Sunny declared

she'd seen everything there was to see in Stoney-brook. "This isn't a bad town," she told us as we lay in the hammock in the backyard after dinner that night. (Dawn and I were lying in the hammock, that is. Sunny was pacing beside it.) "But it's limited. I mean, there are only so many people here, and so many places to see. There's only one museum!"

"The museum is pretty good for a town this size," I said.

"True," agreed Sunny. "But don't you want to see more? Don't you want to see different kinds of people? Cool stores? *Dozens* of museums? Don't you want to experience more than Stoneybrook can offer?"

"Exactly what are you suggesting?" Dawn asked warily.

Sunny just kept pacing.

"Sunny? Tell us what you're planning."

Sunny stopped in her tracks. Her eyes were gleaming with excitement. "I'm planning something amazing," she said. "I'm planning a trip to the most exciting city in the world. Tomorrow. The three of us."

"I don't know if my dad will — " I began.

Sunny shook her head. "This has nothing to do

with your dad," she said. "This is just us. Off to New York for a magical day on our own! And nobody has to know."

"You mean you want us to sneak off to New York?" Dawn asked, her eyes wide.

Sunny nodded. "Bingo."

✳ Chapter 11

Dawn sat up suddenly, and I almost fell out of the hammock.

Sunny didn't seem to notice. She kept pacing.

"Sunny," Dawn said. "You're kidding, right?"

Sunny stopped and looked at us. "Kidding? Why should I be kidding?"

We stared back at her. "You want us to sneak off to New York City by ourselves without telling anyone?" I asked.

"That's the general idea. Why is that such a big deal?"

"It's just — "

"You've been there before on your own, haven't you? With Stacey?"

"Well, yes," I said. "But we had permission. And a plan."

"We can make a plan," Sunny said. "It would be more fun without one, but a plan is fine. And as for permission — " She waved a hand. "That's just a formality. I'm sure they wouldn't mind. But I want to go tomorrow, and if we ask now there'll be one of those long, drawn-out decision processes that parents specialize in. They'll torture us with 'we'll see,' and 'maybe,' and the next thing you know it'll be time for me to head back home to California."

I didn't think she was being fair. Sharon and my dad aren't like that. But I could tell Sunny wasn't going to hear anything I said. She was in her own little Sunny world.

"Sunny," Dawn began. "Sunny, stop pacing and listen to me."

Sunny stopped in her tracks. "Yes, *ma'am*," she said, grinning.

Dawn sighed. She shifted position in the hammock. "Look, I'd love to go to New York. It's a great city, no question about it. And I'd love to show you all the major landmarks, like the Empire State Building and the Statue of Liberty. We could even go to Ellis Island. That is a totally cool place to visit."

Sunny looked unimpressed.

Dawn went on. "But why don't we just wait for

the weekend and make it a family trip? I know my mom would love to go too. Richard always has a good time in the city. And Jeff? He'd have a blast."

She sounded so enthusiastic. I thought for sure Sunny would agree to the plan.

I was wrong.

"Dawn, Dawn, Dawn." Sunny sighed. "You know I adore your family. They've been wonderful to me. So don't take this the wrong way. But that is *so* not what I'm talking about."

Dawn raised her eyebrows. "Oh, no?" She folded her arms across her chest. "Then why don't you tell us what you're talking about, Sunny."

"You don't have to get all bent out of shape," Sunny said lightly. "Come on, this is about fun."

Dawn looked skeptical, but she uncrossed her arms. "I like fun. Go on."

Sunny sat down on the ground next to the hammock. "All right," she said. "Here's the thing. Visiting places like the ones you were talking about is fine for tourists." She paused and held up a hand. "Don't say it," she said before Dawn or I could speak. "I know, I'm visiting from California. That makes me a tourist. And someday I'd love to do the Empire State, World Trade Center, Statue of Liberty tourist thing. But what I'm talking about is different. What I want to do is see the *real* New York. The New York that New Yorkers see."

She jumped to her feet. "Wait a sec," she said. "Don't move." She ran toward the house.

Dawn let out a huge breath and flopped back into the hammock. "*What* is she thinking?" she asked, lying there with her eyes closed.

I shook my head. "I don't know."

"Shh," Dawn warned me. "She's coming back."

Sunny ran across the lawn, waving something at us. As she drew closer, I saw that it was a magazine.

"Check this out," she said, climbing into the hammock with us. She flipped through the pages until she found what she was looking for. Then she held the magazine so we could both see it. "City Chic," blared the headline of the article she'd opened to. "Where Do Real City Kids Shop?" The guy and girl in the picture looked impossibly sophisticated and exotic. He was tall with a dark goatee and short dark hair. His eyes were obscured by yellow-tinted sunglasses. She was even taller than he was, with long corkscrews of coppery-red hair. Both were wearing all-black outfits.

"Look at them. Are they not the coolest?" Sunny was shaking her head.

"They're very cool," Dawn admitted. "But what do they have to do with us?"

Sunny rolled her eyes. "You're not listening, are you? My point is that these kids are real New Yorkers. They don't spend time hanging around the Empire State Building with their parents. They *live* in the city. It's their environment. They know where to go, what to do to have a great time. Shopping is a part of that, but so are restaurants and clubs."

Gulp. "Clubs?" I repeated. "You mean, like, with music and — and everything?"

Sunny patted my hand. "Take a deep breath, Mary Anne. Don't worry. I'm not suggesting anything wild here. But wouldn't you at least like to sneak a peek at the kind of place that kids like these" — she gestured at the magazine — "go to? I mean, these two don't hang out at any boring old mall, if you know what I'm saying."

"I didn't realize you were so bored with our mall," Dawn said stiffly.

"Oh, come on," Sunny answered impatiently. "Admit it. The mall's fine, but do you want to spend every day of your life there?"

"Of course not," I said.

"Then let's go somewhere different!" Sunny exclaimed, jumping out of the hammock.

Dawn and I held on as the hammock careened back and forth. Sunny was pacing again.

"Look. It's not such a big deal," Sunny said. "Tomorrow, as soon as Sharon and Richard leave for work, we'll head for the train station. We take the train to New York, take a cab to the Village, and walk around for a few hours. Then we hop back into a cab, zoom up to the train station, and we're back before anyone knows any better!"

She made it sound so simple. "How did you figure all that out?" I asked.

"By reading this article," Sunny admitted. "That's how the interviewer met up with the kids. She took a train in from the suburbs and trailed along with them while they walked around in the Village and Soho. The Village is in the lower part of the city. It's where all the coolest people have always hung out," Sunny explained.

"I knew that," Dawn said quickly. "I've been there."

"And Soho stands for South of Houston. As in Houston Street, which, by the way, is pronounced House-ton, not Hyoos-ton. It's even cooler than the Village. It's where all the artists used to live and work and show their stuff. Now there are lots of super-hip shops."

"How do you get there from the Village?" I asked.

"We walk!" Sunny crowed. "That's the best part. Soho and the Village run right into each other."

Suddenly, I noticed something. We weren't talking anymore about whether we would or wouldn't go. We were talking about how to *get* where we were going. How had Sunny convinced us without our noticing?

Dawn frowned. "What about Jeff?" she asked. So she wasn't convinced. Not yet.

"He's planning to spend the day at the Pikes'," Sunny said without missing a beat. "He and the triplets are building a fort or something. I heard him ask Sharon for permission. He'll never know we were gone. And just in case anyone ends up looking for us during the day, we can leave a note saying we went to the pool."

Dawn was quiet for a second.

I was too.

I knew it wasn't right. My dad would be furious if he found out. But would he find out? And really, as Sunny said, what was the big deal? I had been to New York before without an adult along. And this trip would be special. Sunny had made it sound very exciting. Her plan was crazy — but it might work. Still . . .

"Look," Sunny finally said, breaking the silence. "I really need this." She met my eyes. "I'm not going to beg, but it would mean a lot to me if you guys would agree to go."

How could I say no when she put it that way? I'd made it clear that I wanted to be there for her. And this was what she needed me for. I looked at Dawn, and I could tell she was thinking the same thing. She gave me a tiny nod.

"Okay," I said quietly. "We'll go."

✳ Chapter 12

What am I doing? What am I doing?
This is nuts! This is nuts!

The thoughts rattled in my brain — in time to the clickety-clack of the train.

Yes, Sunny, Dawn, and I were on our way to New York.

Eek! Ack! I want to go back!

I hadn't slept much the night before. Partly out of excitement, partly out of pure fear. According to Sunny's plan, we'd stayed in bed this morning until we'd heard Sharon and Dad leave the house. That meant Jeff was gone too, since Sharon was dropping him off at the Pikes' on her way to work.

"If we sit down to breakfast with them, they'll be able to tell something's up," Sunny had explained the night before. "I might be able to hide it, but you two — " She shook her head. "You'd give it away in a second. So it's best to lay low until they're gone. Then we'll jump on our bikes and head for the train station."

Sunny had it all figured out. And she was probably right. If my dad had seen my face that morning, he'd have known immediately that I was nervous about something. And if he asked me what was wrong? I would have had to tell him everything. I wouldn't have been able to lie to his face.

So instead, I'd lied in a note (*Sharon — we're at the pool. See you at dinner!*), and now I was sneaking off to New York. Before we'd left, Dawn had made one suggestion I thought was very smart. She had insisted that we tell *somebody* where we were going, "just in case." (I didn't want to think about the awful possibilities that "just in case" covered, so I didn't.) And that morning, she'd called Stacey to let her know our plan.

"What did Stacey say, anyway?" I asked now as the train rocked along.

"She was so jealous!" Dawn reported. "She said if she didn't have a sitting job today she'd come with us. She said we were going to have a blast. And she said we have to go to Canal Jean."

"What's Canal Jean?" I asked.

"I know! I know!" said Sunny, holding up the magazine she'd shown us the night before. "They talk about it in here. I wanted to go there anyway. It's this cool clothing store in Soho. It's *huge*, and they have everything from vintage clothes to trendy stuff, and the prices are supposed to be really good."

"Stacey said it's like the Macy's of Soho," Dawn told me. "She said there are lots of other, cooler stores. But most of them are really expensive and up-scale. Like, they'll have just one perfect little dress for nine hundred dollars. We can check those out, but if we want to buy anything, Canal Jean is the place for people like us."

I could see that Dawn was catching Sunny's enthusiasm. She didn't seem nervous at all. I decided she had the right idea. It was time to forget my fears and enjoy the day.

We spent the rest of the train ride looking over Sunny's magazine and talking about all the places we wanted to see.

"How are we going to get to the Village anyway?" I asked. "Are we going to take the subway?"

"We could," said Sunny doubtfully. "But let's take a taxi. It'll be more fun because we'll be able to see where we're going."

I had the feeling Sunny was a little scared of the subway. Somehow it made me feel better to know Sunny was scared of *something*.

"So, we'll take the taxi right to Canal Jean?" asked Dawn.

"No way!" Sunny cried. "That wouldn't be any fun. Let's just take it to Washington Square Park. That's supposed to be the heart of Greenwich Village. We can walk anywhere we want from there." She showed us the little map featured in the magazine article. "See? Nothing's that far from the park."

The map was small, so it was hard to tell. But Sunny was probably right. Stacey always says that walking is the best way to get around in New York.

So now we had a plan. And somehow that made me feel better. I sat back and enjoyed the rest of the train ride.

The train pulled into Grand Central Station right on time. "This way," I said when we landed on the platform. I led us up the escalator, feeling pretty cool. The station was familiar to me, since I'd taken the train to New York before. Dawn had too, but not for awhile.

Once we hit the street, though, my anxiety returned. For a few seconds, the three of us just stood on the sidewalk, trying to get our bearings. I always forget how *big* New York is, and how many people live and work there. I mean, everywhere you look are all these giant buildings. And the streets — at least the avenues — seem about ten times as wide as the streets in Stoneybrook. Plus, they're filled with traffic. Noisy, fast traffic. There's a constant flow of trucks, buses, taxis, and cars, not to mention the bicyclists and in-line skaters who whiz by. Every single vehicle seems to be honking for no particular reason. Exhaust fumes fill the air, mixing with, in our case, the smell of hot pretzels being sold from a shiny metal pushcart with a big yellow umbrella.

And the people. The sidewalks are *full* of people of every type and description, and most of them are walking quickly, as if they know exactly where they are headed — and know they are late. We saw people of every color and nationality. Women who looked and dressed like models. Homeless men pushing carts full of deposit bottles they'd pulled out of trash cans. Guys who looked as if they spent their lives at the gym, building up their bodies. Indian women in beautiful saris. Hip-hop guys in backward baseball caps and huge baggy jeans.

"Wow," said Sunny, drinking it all in. "Wow."

"It's something, isn't it?" asked Dawn. She looked a little pale.

"It sure is." Sunny took a deep breath. "So, we're taking a taxi, right?"

"Right," Dawn and I agreed.

But how? How were we supposed to make one of the yellow cars, the ones that were flying by in all that traffic, stop for us? I'd seen Stacey hail a cab before. I knew it wasn't that hard. But the traffic was overwhelming. I felt frozen.

Then I saw Sunny take a small step off the curb and hold up her arm.

"Sunny!" I yelled, reaching out to grab her. "Watch out!"

Just then, a taxi veered toward us, finding its way out of the traffic to stop next to us. Sunny grinned at me. "How about that?" she asked.

We opened the door and climbed into the backseat. "Washington Square Park, please," Sunny said, as cool as a cucumber.

"Sunny!" I said as soon as the cab had lurched away from the curb. "How did you know how to do that?"

"I watched a woman up the block," Sunny confessed. "Plus, I've seen it in movies."

I was impressed.

The cabdriver looked at us in his rearview mirror. "Where are you girls from?" he asked.

"Connecticut," we chorused.

"Well, California," Sunny added. "This is my first time in New York City."

"You girls look a little young to be here by yourselves," said the cabbie, eyeing us again. He was about my dad's age. "You be careful, hear?"

"We will," Dawn promised.

I stared out the window as we whizzed through the busy streets. I almost felt dizzy trying to take in so much at once. I had no idea which direction we were heading. All I knew was that we seemed to be heading there very, very fast. Cabbies in New York are not known for being cautious drivers.

"This where you wanted to go?" asked the driver, a few minutes later. He'd pulled over to one side of a wide avenue (Fifth Avenue, I realized later). Straight ahead and across a side street was a huge, beautiful gray stone arch, and beyond the arch was a park full of people.

"Definitely!" cried Sunny. She was practically bouncing up and down in her seat with excitement.

We paid the driver (I knew enough from other visits to remember that we were supposed to tip him, so I added a dollar to the amount on the meter) and climbed out of the cab.

"Yesss!" Sunny stood staring at the park, a broad

smile on her face. "This is *exactly* why I wanted to come here." She looked both ways, then trotted across the street. Dawn and I trotted behind her. "Check this *out*!" Sunny was entranced. "Talk about finding you a city boyfriend, Mary Anne — this would definitely be the place." Her eyes followed a skateboard dude who zipped by, wearing a pair of low-slung shorts. "Nice tattoos," she said, loudly enough for the boy to hear her. He glanced at her and grinned.

The park was full of activity. Didn't anybody in the city *work*? What were all these people doing hanging out in a park in the middle of the day? The focus of the park was a fountain, and it was surrounded by people: skateboarders, guys playing drums, a juggler, parents pushing strollers, couples kissing, old men feeding pigeons. People strolled up and down the paved paths that crisscrossed the park. Along one side of the park, beneath some trees, were stone tables. At every one, two people were sitting across from each other, playing chess. Other people sat nearby, watching the games and making comments.

Dawn and Sunny and I found seats on a bench near the fountain. For awhile, we just sat and looked at everything going on around us.

"I could sit here and watch all day," Dawn said.

"Me too." I had to agree.

"Not me!" exclaimed Sunny. "I mean, it's incredibly cool here. But there's so much to see! Let's start walking."

I didn't mind. "Okay. Which way to Canal Jean?"

"Oh, let's not rush down there," said Sunny. "Let's just wander for awhile. Let's go . . . down that street!" She waved toward a quiet street on the other side of the park.

"Why not?" asked Dawn with a shrug. I couldn't think of an answer. So we began to wander.

We walked for a long, long time, up one street and down another. I can't even begin to tell you all the things we saw, but here's a partial list:

— An Italian bakery that looked as if it had been there for a hundred years. The bread smelled delicious as we walked by.

— A girl who had short red hair — and I mean *red*, like a red Lifesaver — with black-and-white quills sticking up all over it.

— Tree-lined streets with old brick buildings that sported window boxes overflowing with flowers.

— A very cool-looking mother, all dressed in black and yakking on her cell phone as she pushed a stroller. The baby riding in it was all dressed in black too. New Yorkers like black.

— A guy wearing knee-high leopard-skin boots.

— A store full of all kinds of things made out of glass, including glass candy kisses (I wanted to get one for Claudia, but they were too expensive).

— Guys who looked like pros playing basketball on a street-corner court, with spectators lining every inch of the fence.

— A store full of rugs and Egyptian jewelry, where two purring black-and-white cats seemed to rule (they lived there, according to a sign on the door).

We walked for blocks and blocks, stopping in every store that looked interesting. One whole street was full of nothing but shoe stores! We didn't buy anything; the choices were just too overwhelming. It was fun to look, though.

Until, suddenly, we realized we were starving. It was time to take a break for lunch.

"This looks like a nice place," said Sunny, gesturing toward a cafe with tables on the sidewalk. "What do you think?"

"I'm too exhausted to think," said Dawn.

"And I'm too hungry." I led us to one of the tables and dropped into a chair. "It looks fine."

A waiter dressed in a white shirt, black pants, and a long white apron approached our table. "Hello, ladies," he said, handing us three menus.

Sunny opened hers and took a look. "Yow!" she exclaimed, dropping it like a hot potato.

❈ Chapter 13

The waiter, still standing there, raised an eyebrow.

"I mean," said Sunny, blushing, "I think this place might be a little out of our price range."

I opened my menu and looked. The cheapest thing I could see was a salad. For fourteen dollars! "I think you're right," I said, cracking up. I looked at Dawn and saw that she was laughing too.

The waiter just smiled, took the menus back, and suggested a pizza place around the corner. We stumbled away from the table, giggling so hard it was difficult to walk.

The pizza was delicious. In fact, it might have been the best pizza I'd ever had. Or maybe it was just that I was so hungry. Anyway, by the time we'd finished scarfing up two slices each, washed down with large sodas, we all felt ready for more walking.

By that time, I was feeling less nervous and more at home. I think Dawn and Sunny were too. We'd become used to keeping one another in view as we walked down the street, even when we were briefly separated by crowds pushing past us. Still, I was glad we'd had the sense to designate a meeting place (under the arch at Washington Square Park) in case we were separated for real.

I was so interested in everything I was seeing, everything we were doing, that I'd even stopped thinking about the fact that we'd come here on our own, without telling our parents. Sunny — and the city — seemed to have cast a spell over me.

"Whoa, check this out!" said Sunny as we strolled by a huge brightly colored mural featuring abstract people dancing to a wild beat.

"Claudia would love that." Dawn stopped to look.

"Claudia would love *this*," I said a few minutes later, when we came across a whole corner full of street vendors. "Look! I think this table has every kind of hair accessory in the universe!" The variety was awesome. There were butterfly clips, dragonfly clips, scarves and headbands and barrettes of every color and type — plus a ton of jewelry: pins featuring every animal and hobby you could think of, earrings and nose rings and toe rings and bracelets and anklets and fake tattoos and necklaces and charm bracelets.

The next stall featured T-shirts and tanks with Chinese characters on them, and the stall next to that was selling mini-backpacks and some really cool tapestry shoulder bags.

We wandered around looking at everything. I couldn't help buying some dragonfly clips. They were so cheap (I don't think anything at that table was more than ten dollars). Dawn and Sunny spent some money too. Dawn bought a shoulder bag and Sunny bought a black Chinese tank top with a red dragon on it.

According to the map in the magazine, we were in Soho by then, and as we continued walking, the mix of stores we saw was incredible. We passed fancy boutiques, expensive home furnishing stores (a set of sheets we saw in one window cost $850 — can you imagine?), and even a surfer-dude clothing store with miniature surfboards for door handles. We passed some art galleries, a spa (you couldn't see anyone getting treatments, just a bright, open space with lots of wood and chrome), another one of those old Italian bakeries, and a store full of things from Tibet.

Finally, we reached Broadway, the street where Canal Jean is located. (Remember Canal Jean? I'd almost forgotten about it, but Sunny hadn't.)

We'd been walking down some relatively quiet streets, but Broadway was *bustling*. It was a wide avenue with lots of traffic. Once again, the sidewalks were full of people. But the stores were a lot less fancy. We went into one, attracted by the music blaring out into the street, and ended up trying on some wild neon-colored wigs.

Finally, Sunny spotted the checkerboard flag that is the Canal Jean logo. We headed into the store, which is *huge*, with several levels, and started to wander around. Dawn hit the vintage clothing area, while Sunny headed for a pile of sailor pants in the army-navy section. I was checking out a cool pair of baggy overalls when I heard a girl next to me ask a nearby salesperson (a guy with a pierced eyebrow and a blond mohawk) what time it was.

"Three-thirty," said the boy.

I nearly fainted. That couldn't be right. I checked my watch.

Mohawk boy was wrong. It wasn't three-thirty.

It was three forty-two.

And if we were going to make it back to Stoneybrook before Sharon and Dad came home from work, we had to head for the train station *now*.

I ran to where Dawn was searching through a rack of skirts and told her. Together, we went in search of Sunny.

We found her near the entrance. "Hey, you guys! Check this out." She held up a flier. "This club sounds like a blast. They're having a battle of the bands tonight."

"Club?" I stared at her.

"Tonight?" Dawn looked shocked too. "Sunny, we have to be *home* tonight. In fact, we have to be home in a couple of hours. We should be leaving now."

"What are you talking about? We finally made it to this store, and I haven't even had a chance to look around."

Dawn and I exchanged a glance. Sunny was only going to get stubborn if we tried to force the issue. "We can look around a little," I said. "But then we have to grab a taxi and head back to the train station."

Sunny made a face. "Oh, come on," she said.

"We have time. Besides, I'm hungry again. And I really think we should check out this club."

"Sunny, my dad will be home from work in less than three hours," I said.

"So? You left a note saying we're at the pool, right? It doesn't close until later. He'll never know." She stood up and started to walk toward the stairs to the upper level. "We're here to have fun, remember?" she tossed over her shoulder. "If you guys want to spend your time worrying, that's fine. I'm going to enjoy myself."

I saw Dawn's face turn red.

"Sunny Winslow," she said in a deathly quiet voice. Nobody else in the store turned to look, but Sunny stopped in her tracks. She turned to face Dawn.

"Yes, Dawn Schafer?" she asked in a teasing voice.

Dawn did not crack a smile. "I've had enough of this," she said.

"Enough of what, exactly? Enough of what, Dawn?"

"Let's go outside, you guys," I said. I had the feeling a big scene was coming.

They both ignored me. "Sunny, I'm just going to say this once," Dawn said. "It's time to go."

"No way. I'm having an awesome time, and I'm not ready to go. If you're so worried about getting home, why don't you go ahead and leave? I'll be just fine on my own."

Dawn's face turned an even darker shade of red. "That's not how it works, Sunny. I'm not leaving you in this city on your own. We came together, and we're leaving together."

"Then we're not leaving now," Sunny said airily. She turned to watch as a shopper walked by, dressed in an off-the-shoulder sequined pink prom gown. (The shopper was a guy!)

I stared at her. I couldn't believe my ears. I had no idea how to handle Sunny, so I let Dawn do the talking.

"That's it, Sunny," Dawn said. "I've had it. You are the most selfish person I've ever met. My family and I have humored you for the last two weeks. And how do you pay us back? By dragging Mary Anne and me into doing something we *know* is wrong."

"Oh, right. I dragged you." Sunny rolled her eyes. "Up until a few minutes ago, you guys were having a blast. Now I'm my own evil twin for forcing you to come here."

Dawn shook her head. "You don't get it, do you?

The point is, you've been getting your own way ever since — for a long time now."

"Oh, just say it," said Sunny. "Ever since my mother died. Is that what you mean?"

Suddenly, I couldn't hear any of the noise around me. It was as if the whole store had gone silent. I drew in a breath, shocked. Dawn's face went from red to white.

Sunny forced a grin. "Is it?" she asked.

Finally, Dawn nodded. "Yes, Sunny, that's what I mean."

Once again, I remembered how much Mrs. Winslow's death must have affected Dawn. I could see it in her face. She had all her own grief to deal with, and here she was, trying her best to make Sunny's visit a good one. Dawn, I realized, had probably come back to Stoneybrook hoping to sort out her own emotions, but she hadn't had time to do that. Every minute had been taken up with frantic activity, all to suit Sunny.

"You guys," I said, stepping forward.

Dawn didn't even seem to hear me. She was looking at Sunny. "Just because you're having a hard time doesn't mean you have a right to treat everyone else badly. Things can't always go your way."

Sunny tossed her head. "You think things go my way?" she asked, her voice hard. "Like when my mom died? Was that having things go my way?"

"That's not fair," Dawn said in a whisper.

"Oh, so what." Sunny sounded disgusted. "Life is not fair. And, of all people, I should know." She turned on her heel. "Forget it," she said. "Let's go back to safe old Connecticut." She walked toward the exit.

Dawn and I stood still for a second. Then we followed Sunny back out onto Broadway.

We found a cab and took it to the train station. We made it onto a Stoneybrook-bound train with minutes to spare. And we rode the whole way home without any one of us speaking a single word.

❋ Chapter 14

We made it back in time — *just* in time. I think Sharon's car pulled into the driveway about eight minutes after we'd walked into the house.

Can I just say, right now, right here, that I will *never* do anything so stupid again? It was *so* not a good idea to go to New York without our parents' permission. We were very lucky nothing happened to us, and very *very* lucky to have gotten away with it.

Anyway . . . we still hadn't spoken to one another by the time we got home. Dawn threw her new shoulder bag down on the kitchen table (I picked it up and set it aside before Sharon or Richard could spot it and ask about it) and slammed out the door. I knew she was headed over to the Pikes' to pick up Jeff. Sunny stomped upstairs to their room and slammed *that* door.

Me? I just stood in the kitchen, wondering what to do. When I heard Sharon's car, I panicked. I wasn't ready to face her, but there wasn't time to run to my room. So I opened the fridge and stuck my head inside.

"Hi, sweetie," said Sharon as she entered the kitchen. "Have a good day?"

"Sure."

"What are you doing?"

"Just checking to see what we might have for supper. How about a salad and — "

"I thought we'd order pizza tonight," Sharon interrupted. "I had a long day and I'm too tired to cook."

"We had — " I stopped myself before I could say we'd had pizza for lunch. They don't sell pizza at the pool. "We had a long day too," I said, trying to cover my mistake.

Sharon laughed. She thought I was joking.

I laughed too. "Pizza sounds great." I didn't care *what* we had for dinner. I just wanted to be out of that kitchen before I gave something away. I closed the fridge and told Sharon I'd be upstairs until suppertime.

"See you," she said vaguely, waving a hand in my direction. She'd collapsed into a chair and was looking through the day's mail.

I climbed the stairs, suddenly exhausted. I felt as if I could crawl into bed right then and sleep until morning. The door to Dawn and Sunny's room was closed. I wondered if Sunny was still furious.

Then I heard it.

A loud sniff. A sob. Another sniff.

Sunny was crying.

That was something new.

Gently, I knocked on the door.

"Go away!"

"Sunny," I said, leaning my head against the door. That's all I said. There was just a little pause. Then Sunny spoke again, and this time she wasn't yelling.

"Mary Anne?" I heard a sob in her voice. "Could you — come in?"

I pushed the door open.

Sunny was huddled on her bed, hugging her pillow and looking about five years old. She let out a sob.

I hugged her. Then I sat on the bed and patted her back while she cried and cried.

Did you ever start crying about one thing and end up crying about every single thing that wasn't right in your life? That kind of crying can require a *lot* of tears. I had the feeling that's what Sunny was doing. She was crying about what had happened between her and Dawn, and about her mom dying, and about her father being so busy with his store, and about — *everything*. I just sat there with her as she sobbed. Once in awhile I said something soothing like, "It's okay."

Sunny cried and cried until finally, she seemed to be all cried out.

I stood up and grabbed a box of tissues off her bureau. "Here," I said. "Blow your nose and wipe your eyes." I felt almost as if Sunny were one of my baby-sitting charges.

She took the tissues gratefully. "Thanks," she said. She sniffed and let out a big sigh.

"I know," I said. "I think you needed that."

She nodded. "Mary Anne, I'm really sorry," she said.

"Don't be sorry. Crying is okay. It's more than okay. It's good."

"Not about the crying." Sunny shook her head. "I mean, I'm sorry about dragging you to New York. I know you only went along to humor me. I took advantage of that. I made you do something you didn't want to do."

I shrugged. "I agreed to go," I told her. "It's not

your fault. I could have said no. Anyway, it's okay. I know your mind has been on other things."

"I wish." Sunny sounded bitter. "I wish my mind were anywhere else but — but in my mind." She shook her head. "That doesn't make sense. What I mean is, I came here to Stoneybrook because I wanted a change. I wanted to get away from all the things on my mind. But you know what?"

"What?"

"Only my environment changed. I mean, Connecticut and California couldn't be more different. But even though everything around me is unfamiliar, none of the other stuff has changed. My life is what it is. Facts are facts."

"I know," I said, meeting her eyes.

"I can't imagine what I was thinking," Sunny went on. "I guess I thought that if I kept busy enough, I wouldn't have to deal with the facts." She looked down at the tissue in her hands. She'd been wringing it, and it was shredded. "It didn't work." I saw a few last tears slip down her cheeks.

I handed her a new tissue.

"I was silly to think it would," she said after she'd blown her nose again.

"No. Not silly. You were just — wishing."

She glanced up at me, a question in her eyes.

"I've wished for things too," I confessed.

"Like, that your mom hadn't died?"

I nodded. "Like that."

We looked at each other for a moment.

"Mary Anne? What's it like not to have a mother?"

I took a deep breath. "What's it like? I don't know. I don't know what it's like to *have* one, so I don't know how to compare."

Sunny didn't say anything. I saw that she wanted a better answer than that.

"Okay. Here's what it's like. It's like — it's like you're missing a big piece of yourself. You can still survive in the world. You can be happy and have a great life. But there's always this thing you come back to, this piece that's missing. This piece that almost everyone else seems to have and take for granted."

Sunny nodded. "You know, my dad loves me a lot. And so does my aunt. But my mom and I — we had something special. I miss that."

"You'll never stop missing that. Or her," I said. "I'm pretty sure about that. But I also know that it won't always hurt the way it does now."

Downstairs I heard a door open and close. Dawn

and Jeff must have been back. But Dawn didn't come upstairs. She was probably still angry with Sunny.

Sunny sat up in her bed, clutching the tissue. "I don't mind how much it hurts, really," she said. "In a way, I'm more afraid of forgetting her." She turned her face away for a second. "Sometimes," she whispered, "I already have a hard time remembering what she looked like."

"It's okay," I said, patting her back. "Really. She's in your heart for always. You'll never forget her. You don't have to worry about that."

Sunny cried some more. Once she'd started, she couldn't seem to stop. I just sat beside her, patting her back and handing her tissues. Finally, her sobs subsided again. "I think I've made a really big decision about something," she said.

"What?"

"I think I need to go back to California. I need to go home."

"Really?"

She nodded. "My dad misses me, and I miss him. I think we need to be together right now. And anyway, being here just doesn't feel right. It's like being in a holding pattern. You know what I mean by that? Like when you're in an airplane that can't land because the airport's too busy. So you just circle and circle, waiting for something to change. That's a holding pattern. I need to move forward."

I could tell Sunny was serious about leaving, and I had the feeling it was a good idea for her to go. "You're probably right," I told her. "But we'll miss you." It was true. Having Sunny around had been exhausting, but it had been exhilarating too. And I'd come to like her. A lot.

"How am I going to tell Dawn?" Sunny asked.

"You don't have to."

We looked up and saw Dawn standing in the doorway. She must have been there for a couple of minutes without our noticing. She sat down on the bed and reached out to hug Sunny.

Their fight was over. Neither of them had to say a word. It was just understood.

Sunny had figured out what she really needed to do. And this time, Dawn and I could support her all the way.

✱ Chapter 15

"Are you sure?" Sharon asked Sunny later that night when Sunny explained that she wanted to go back to California.

Sunny nodded. "I'll miss it here," she said. "You've all been really great to me. But it's time to go home."

My dad nodded. "I can understand that," he said. "Have you told your father yet?"

Sunny nodded again. "I already called him. I think he was pretty glad to hear it." She looked down at her hands. "He says he's missed me."

"I'm sure he has," said Sharon. "And now we will. How soon do you want to leave?"

"I was thinking Sunday," said Sunny. "Two days after tomorrow. My dad made some calls already and there's a flight, if you can take me to the airport."

"Of course." Sharon smiled. "How about if we have a party for you on Saturday night? It can be a going-away party, plus a housewarming party for us. We have lots of friends and neighbors who are dying to see how the house turned out."

It was an excellent idea. There wasn't much time to pull together a party, but we had that Sunny energy on our side. We spent the next two days running around like crazy. We planned a menu, shopped for groceries, baked some healthy but yummy carob-chip cookies and two peach pies, tidied up the house, and made at least a dozen phone calls to invite people.

Sunny, Dawn, and I worked easily together, talking and laughing. I didn't feel left out anymore, even when Sunny and Dawn talked about California friends. Sunny and I had bonded, and I knew we'd always have that.

"Should we invite Cole and his friends?" I asked Sunny teasingly at one point.

Sunny just shook her head. "Sorry about that. You seem to be doing just fine without a boyfriend. Don't rush into anything, okay?"

Late Saturday afternoon, we decorated the backyard with strings of little white lights. The weather was beautiful, so we set up tables near the herb garden and covered them with mismatched tablecloths we borrowed from the neighbors. My dad helped get the barbecue grill ready to go, and we filled two tubs with ice and stocked them with cans of soda.

We finished everything about ten minutes before the guests were due to arrive. Then we changed our clothes and headed back downstairs to greet our friends.

Kristy and Abby Stevenson (another honorary BSC member) were the first to arrive. "Wow, everything looks great," said Kristy.

I had to admit she was right. The barn doors were wide open, and you could see that the big butcher block counter in the kitchen was covered with food waiting to be served outside. The lights in the garden were on, even though it wasn't dark yet. "Thanks," I said, feeling proud.

I saw Abby approach Sunny. "Hi," she said. "I'm sorry you're leaving before we got to hang out much. And — I wanted to say how sorry I am about your mother."

Sunny nodded. "Thanks," she said. "That means a lot."

I was impressed — by two things. First of all, that Abby seemed to know exactly what to say to

Sunny. I guess that's because she lost a parent too; her dad died in a car accident only a few years ago. And second, that Sunny responded the way she did. A few days ago, I wouldn't have been surprised to hear her change the subject or try to make some kind of joke. This was a new Sunny, a Sunny who was facing her feelings. In a funny way, I felt proud of her.

Within half an hour, the party was in full swing. Stacey and Claudia had arrived, and so had the Pikes, including Mallory, who was back from camp. "This is like a BSC reunion," she said. Her brothers ran off to find Jeff and raid the dessert table.

I was feeling hungry myself by then. "Let's eat," I suggested. I didn't have to say more than that. Soon we were loading up plates, grabbing burgers off the grill, and setting ourselves up under the apple tree for a big feast.

As we were choosing sodas, I heard Stacey admiring Sunny's tank top — the one she'd bought in New York. "I love it," she said. "It looks new. Where'd you find it? It doesn't look like it came from Washington Mall."

"It didn't. It came from — " Sunny looked around and caught herself. Sharon was standing nearby, spooning potato salad onto someone's plate.

Sunny gave a little cough. "I've had it for awhile," she finished lamely.

Stacey just smiled. I think she guessed the truth.

We ate until we were stuffed. Then we just lay there talking. Claudia disappeared for awhile and returned grinning. "I love your room," she told me. "Great colors."

"When did you see it?" I asked. "I was planning to give you guys a tour in a little bit."

"Jeff beat you to it," Claudia told me. She pointed to a cluster of people near the house. "He's offering tours of the house for twenty-five cents. Thirty-five if you want to see his room."

Dawn and I looked at each other and cracked up.

"It's a good business," said Claudia. "There are plenty of people here who haven't seen the house yet. And he gives a very thorough tour."

"It's true," put in Abby. "The house looks great, by the way."

"You too?" I asked.

"I was with the first group to go through," she said, grinning.

Dawn shook her head. "I suppose I should tell Mom, but you know what? She probably wouldn't be mad. She'd be happy that Jeff likes the house well enough to show it off."

"Still, he shouldn't be charging the guests," I said.

"How about if I distract him by organizing a softball game?" Kristy asked, jumping to her feet. "I brought a bunch of gear just in case anyone wanted to play."

The party lasted well into the evening. Just about everyone joined in the game, and we played until it was too dark to see. By then the tiny white lights in the garden looked beautiful, and so did the big square of light from the wide kitchen doors. As our guests left, almost every one of them said something about how lovely our new home was.

I had to agree.

Later, Dawn and I helped Sunny with her packing. It didn't take long. She threw things into her duffel without much thought. All except for those notebooks, her mother's journals. "Sometime I'd like to show you these," she told me as she laid them gently on top of her clothes.

"I'd love to see them," I said.

After awhile, I could tell Dawn and Sunny needed a little time alone to say good-bye, so I headed off to bed. Before I fell asleep, I heard a knock at my door.

"Mary Anne?" It was Sunny. "I just wanted to

say good night," she said. "And — I wanted to thank you. You really helped me."

She sat on my bed and we talked for awhile. It was late, and everyone else was asleep. The house was very quiet.

Then I began to hear the strangest noises. Creaking sounds, coming from all around. I'd heard them before as I was drifting off to sleep, but they'd never seemed so loud. "What's that?" I asked, startled.

"It's the house settling," said Sunny. "My house makes the same sounds sometimes. It just means that the house is taking its shape, settling in."

After she'd reassured me, Sunny said good night and left.

The next morning we headed for the airport. Dawn and Sunny sat in the backseat, talking about plans for later that summer when Dawn would return to California. I sat up front with Sharon.

Seeing Sunny off was sad. But I felt happy for her too. "She's doing the right thing," I said to Dawn as we watched Sunny walk toward her gate.

That night, I lay in bed thinking about the last couple of weeks. They'd been busy ones, full of change. But now everything seemed to be settling into place. Sunny had gone home. Jeff was feeling as if he had a home away from home. And me? I thought about how proud I'd felt when our guests told me they liked our house. I thought about how comfortable I was in my room, how easy the house was to live in, how seldom I'd thought about our old house in the last few days. I looked down at Tigger, lying peacefully next to my pillow. And I sighed. It was as if I'd finally found the ruby slippers and clicked my heels.

I was home.

As I drifted off to sleep, I heard those creaking noises again. But this time they didn't startle me or scare me. They were just the sound of the house settling, the sound of my new home taking shape around me.

Ann M. Martin

About the Author

ANN MATTHEWS MARTIN was born on August 12, 1955. She grew up in Princeton, NJ, with her parents and her younger sister, Jane.

Although Ann used to be a teacher and then an editor of children's books, she's now a full-time writer. She gets ideas for her books from many different places. Some are based on personal experiences. Others are based on childhood memories and feelings. Many are written about contemporary problems or events.

All of Ann's characters, even the members of the Baby-sitters Club, are made up. (So is Stoneybrook.) But many of her characters are based on real people. Sometimes Ann names her characters after people she knows; other times she chooses names she likes.

In addition to the Baby-sitters Club books, Ann Martin has written many other books for children. Her favorite is *Ten Kids, No Pets* because she loves big families and she loves animals. Her favorite BSC book is *Kristy's Big Day*. (Kristy is her favorite baby-sitter.)

Ann M. Martin now lives in New York with her cats, Gussie, Woody, and Willy, and her dog, Sadie. Her hobbies are reading, sewing, and needlework — especially making clothes for children.

Look for #12

CLAUDIA AND THE DISASTER DATE

We rode to my house in silence.

"Thanks," I said when I got out. "It was fun."

"It was?" Alan said. I had the sudden, uncomfortable feeling that he knew exactly what I was thinking.

But that wasn't possible. Was it?

"See you later," I went on.

"I hope so," said Alan. But his voice was cool, careful. Very un-Alan.

I hurried into the house. The car pulled away.

Upstairs in my room, I flopped on my bed. I'd been on worse dates, but few that had felt so awkward. How had that happened? Up until tonight, I'd enjoyed Alan's company and I was pretty sure he had enjoyed mine.

But tonight, he'd been stiff, awkward. And that had made me feel the same way.

Or did I make Alan feel weird? Had he picked up on my nervousness about being seen with him?

That would be a first, I told myself. Someone else making weird Alan feel weird.

I knew I wasn't being fair. But I was tired. And confused. How could I go out with somebody if I always had to worry about what he might do, or what other people might think?

It wasn't worth it.

It just wasn't worth it.

I told myself that over and over until I finally fell asleep.